"I don't suppose y⊔ ⊔day **about the missing camper.**

"Not a thing."

"Or the woman we found in the woods?"

"Not yet. It'll take time to identify her."

"When we discovered her, you said 'not again.' What did you mean?"

His jaw tightened, and his gaze shifted to the side. Several seconds passed in silence. Finally, he spoke. "Three months ago, I worked a case where a woman disappeared from Milligan. Her car was abandoned at the edge of a wooded area along Route 90. She was found near Pensacola two days later. Same shape as the woman we found."

Head smashed in with a blunt object, maybe a hammer. "The case you worked, the lady was dark-haired and slender, like our Julia Morris?"

He nodded, his expression grim. "The first victim and now the woman we discovered. If we find that Julia Morris met the same end..."

She finished the thought for him. "You have a serial killer on your hands."

He opened his mouth as if to say something else, then stopped. But she didn't need him to voice the thought aloud. She could see it in his eyes.

"Dark hair, slender, physically fit. I match the profile..."

Carol J. Post writes fun and fast-paced inspirational romantic suspense stories and lives in the beautiful mountains of North Carolina. She plays the piano and also enjoys sailing, hiking and camping—almost anything outdoors. Her daughters and grandkids live too far away for her liking, so she now pours all that nurturing into taking care of two highly spoiled black cats.

Books by Carol J. Post

Love Inspired Suspense

Midnight Shadows
Motive for Murder
Out for Justice
Shattered Haven
Hidden Identity
Mistletoe Justice
Buried Memories
Reunited by Danger
Fatal Recall
Lethal Legacy
Bodyguard for Christmas
Dangerous Relations
Trailing a Killer

Canine Defense

Searching for Evidence
Sniffing Out Justice

Visit the Author Profile page
at LoveInspired.com for more titles.

Sniffing Out Justice

CAROL J. POST

LOVE INSPIRED SUSPENSE
INSPIRATIONAL ROMANCE

LOVE INSPIRED® SUSPENSE
INSPIRATIONAL ROMANCE

ISBN-13: 978-1-335-48391-1

Sniffing Out Justice

Recycling programs
for this product may
not exist in your area.

Love Inspired
22 Adelaide St. West, 41st Floor
Toronto, Ontario M5H 4E3, Canada
www.LoveInspired.com

Printed in U.S.A.

Fear thou not; for I am with thee: be not dismayed;
for I am thy God: I will strengthen thee;
yea, I will help thee; yea, I will uphold thee
with the right hand of my righteousness.
—*Isaiah* 41:10

Thanks to my sister, Kimberly Coker, for helping me plot my books and being the navigator on all my research trips. You're the best sis ever!

Thank you to my editor, Katie Gowrie, and my critique partners, Karen Fleming and Sabrina Jarema, for making my stories the best they can be.

And thank you to my husband, Chris, for your unending love, encouragement and support. Thanks for all the things you do, too, like making sure I have clean clothes and something to eat when I'm on deadline and buying me chocolate. After forty-three years, I'd still do it all over again.

ONE

The sun shone from low in the eastern sky, casting long shadows over the group gathered at the edge of the parking lot. Beyond the Blackwater River State Park campground lay hundreds of acres of pine forests, swamps and scrubby ridges. Somewhere in that vastness of nature, a twenty-six-year-old woman had disappeared.

Kristina Ashbaugh-Richards swiped a hand across her forehead, slick with beads of sweat. At barely nine in the morning, it was already hot and humid. Of course, Florida was always hot and humid in early August, even in the Panhandle. Her T-shirt was damp where her pack rested against her back, and she was looking forward to shedding the hiking boots she'd put on an hour and a half earlier.

She took a swig from her water bottle. One end of a leash circled her wrist, the other end attached to her golden retriever's collar. Bella wasn't the only dog there. Almost forty Escambia County search and rescue volunteers had gathered, about half of them with a canine partner.

Three people stood in the center of the semicircle of volunteers, one holding a stack of papers. She'd introduced herself as Teresa. "The info on our lady is all here, including a picture."

She handed the stack to the gentleman next to her. "Eddie's going to give one to each of you. You're looking for Julia Morris—dark hair, shoulder length. She's slender, in good shape, enjoys the outdoors. A week ago yesterday, she left her home in Fort Walton Beach to do some wilderness camping in the Blackwater Forest, a nature photography trip. She was to report back to work Monday morning. When she didn't, her coworkers got concerned and called the authorities. She apparently never made it home from that camping trip."

Kris reached down to scratch the top of Bella's head. The dog was standing at attention in her black-and-orange vest, Search & Rescue printed across both sides. Her muscles were stiff with anticipation. This was their first search and rescue mission in more than a year and a half. Though it had been a while, Bella obviously hadn't forgotten. Nothing brought working dogs more satisfaction than participating and succeeding in what they were trained to do.

After assigning grids to the volunteers and giving them items of the missing camper's clothing, those in charge released them to begin. Bella strained at the leash, eager to start the search, and Kris's pulse picked up speed. She'd stayed away far too long.

After she'd taken a few steps, someone spoke a short distance behind her. "Glad I caught you. Sorry I'm late."

The male voice brushed her mind with a vague sense of familiarity. She cast a glance over her shoulder but couldn't see past the others in the party.

"Glad you made it. I'll team you up with Kristina Richards and her dog, Bella."

At Teresa's words, Kris gave a tug on the leash. "Hold on, Bella."

She waited for the others to disperse. When the newcomer turned to face her, her stomach did a free fall, then tightened into a solid knot.

His jaw went slack, but he recovered instantly. A slow, easy smile spread across his face. He'd always had an infectious smile. She wasn't susceptible anymore.

Kris squared her shoulders as Teresa led him in her direction.

"Tony, this is Kristina Richards and her dog, Bella. Tony Sanderson."

Tony nodded. "We've met. We were friends through high school, then lost touch."

Friends. Was that what he called it?

"Great. I'll let you get on your way."

Kris set out again, letting Tony fall in next to her. She wouldn't wait on him, although she likely wouldn't have to. He looked like he could keep up with her just fine, even on her morning runs. He'd filled out nicely since high school, but other than that and how the lines of his face had grown more mature, he hadn't changed a lot. His sandy blond hair was as thick as ever, and those deep brown eyes still seemed to hold a hint of humor.

"How have you been?" His question cut across her thoughts.

"Okay." She focused her gaze straight ahead. She wouldn't make small talk. "How much do you know about what we're doing today?"

"I know we're looking for a young woman who never returned from a wilderness camping trip. What else can you tell me?"

She removed the paper she'd folded and stuffed into her pocket. "Here's her information. She was reported missing after she didn't show up for work yesterday."

He read what she handed him and passed it back. "Where are we headed?"

"We take the catwalk, then head northeast into the woods. Since she was off-grid, no one knows where she set up camp. She left her phone in her car, probably figuring she wouldn't have service anyway."

Several minutes passed in silence before he spoke again. "So, you're Richards now. You're married?"

"No." He'd probably assume she was divorced and hadn't taken back her maiden name. She wouldn't bother to correct him. She wouldn't ask if he was married, either, because she really didn't care.

She'd work with him, though, and not let their past interfere with the job they had to do. A young woman was counting on them. Even if they were paired up on future searches, she'd deal with it professionally.

As they moved along the catwalk, they were silent except for the clomp of their shoes against the wooden planks. Bella trotted as far ahead as the leash would allow, tail wagging. Sounds of the swamp surrounded them—the calls of birds, the buzz of insects and the occasional croak of an alligator.

When the catwalk ended, Kris consulted her GPS and headed into the woods. A rustle sounded some distance to their right, likely one or two of the other volunteers. Her own search area was still some distance away.

Finally, she checked her GPS again and gave Tony a nod. "We're getting close."

She knelt next to Bella and held the T-shirt she'd been given in front of the golden retriever's face. After the dog gave it several sniffs, Kris straightened. "Bella, search."

The dog's demeanor shot from carefree to focused. She moved forward, nose sniffing the air, head swinging side to side as she tried to pick up the scent. Kris led her in a broad zigzag pattern, covering the area thoroughly. Watching her dog wrapped up in the joy of the search, she could almost pretend they were alone.

Until Tony broke the silence. "I love watching these canines do their thing. How long have you had Bella?"

At the mention of her dog, some of the prickliness subsided. "Five years."

"Have you been doing this all that time?"

"No. Bella finished her training three years ago."

"I just joined the group last year, after I moved from Fort Walton Beach to Pensacola."

Great. They were living in the same town again. "I figured you'd want to be closer to Sanderson Charters." She managed to suppress the disdainful nose crinkle that usually accompanied her saying the name. When their dads had parted ways, Tony's had opened a competing business an hour away and took a lot of Ashbaugh customers with him.

"I'm not working in the charter business. I went into police work instead. Dad was a little disappointed, but Nick's doing the business with him, so it all worked out."

She nodded. She'd known Nick, too.

He'd been a year ahead of them in school. Apparently, Tony's big brother didn't have the same moral standards Tony did.

She dipped her gaze to the ground. All the while he was badmouthing Jerry Sanderson, her father had had no right to talk. He was now doing prison time for drug running while Kris and her twin, Kassie, were managing his charter business.

Morning slid into afternoon with no success, and Kris slipped the backpack straps from her shoulders. "I'm starved. How about we take a break?"

"You won't get any argument from me."

While she took a bowl from her pack and filled it with water, Tony sat on a downed tree trunk and removed a sandwich from his own pack. He was dressed in khaki shorts, making her wish she'd opted for something cooler than jeans. At his right hip, the bulge of a holster was barely apparent under his T-shirt. Although she felt comfortable in the woods, having an armed escort couldn't be a bad thing.

Kris refilled Bella's empty bowl with

kibble and removed her own sandwich from its plastic bag. By then, Tony was halfway through his.

He patted the log. "Have a seat."

After sinking onto the rough bark, she bit into her sandwich. Peanut butter and honey had never tasted so good.

Tony took a long swig of water. "From what I've seen, the dogs get discouraged when they search all day and don't find anything."

"They do. Sometimes we'll hide something and have them find it, so they can feel like they did a good job."

He held out a hand, palm up. "Is it okay if I pet her?"

"Sure."

Bella approached, and he scratched her cheek. After downing the last bite of his sandwich, he gave her a two-handed rubdown. "I always enjoy seeing the K-9 officers with their dogs."

"What agency do you work for?"

"Pensacola P.D."

"Do you know Jared Miles?"

"We've met. He's in patrol, isn't he?"

"Yeah."

"I'm in criminal investigations. I take it you know him."

"He's my sister's fiancé."

"Kassie or Alyssa?"

"Kassie. Alyssa took off after she turned eighteen and hasn't been back since. We don't hear much from her." Unless she needed money.

Oh, yeah. She wasn't going to converse with him beyond what was necessary to complete their assigned task. Unfortunately, it was too easy to slip back into the camaraderie they'd shared as teenagers, before he'd humiliated her in front of the entire student body.

Kris finished her sandwich and returned the baggie and other items to her pack. They'd just started out again when the radio she carried crackled to life. One of the dogs had picked up a trail.

Tony looked at her. "We keep searching, right?"

"Yes. We should know something soon."

Soon ended up being less than twenty minutes later. The dog lost the trail at the Blackwater River. Moving a good distance in either direction produced nothing. Neither did crossing the river and searching the other side. Their camper either swam downriver or left in a boat.

They continued their search, moving deeper into the woods. The air hung heavy and damp with Florida's relentless summertime humidity. A breeze moved past them, then disappeared again.

Kris wrinkled her nose. "Ugh. Smell that?"

"There's a dead animal nearby."

Over the next several minutes, the odor grew stronger.

Tony waved a hand in front of his face. "That's bigger than a squirrel or armadillo."

Kris stepped around a tree and looked to her left. Her chest clenched. Her mouth worked, but nothing came out because her throat had closed up.

She grasped Tony's upper arm. He looked

at her, then beyond her. His eyes widened, and his jaw went slack for the second time that day.

Whispered words escaped his mouth, barely audible— "Not again."

He moved closer to the body, and she did, too, because she couldn't seem to extricate her fingers from his biceps. A breeze rustled the trees around them, sweeping away some of the stench of death, and thunder rumbled far in the distance.

She swallowed the bile rising in her throat. Someone had taken a hammer—or something—to the side of their camper's head. Dried blood matted the dark brown hair, and pieces of bone and tissue protruded from the crater.

She squeezed her eyes shut and pressed a shaking hand to her mouth. Tony wrapped an arm around her and led her a few yards away. When he stopped, he still didn't release her. As soon as her legs no longer felt as if they'd buckle, she would step away.

She shook her head. "Why didn't Bella pick up the scent?"

"She's not a cadaver dog, is she?"

"You mean the woman was killed somewhere else and dumped here?"

"I don't know. That's not our camper, though."

"She fits the description."

"This body has been here for at least ten days. But we need to call this in."

She stepped to the side, and he let his arm fall. While he radioed what they'd found, she knelt on the ground, arms wrapped around Bella's body, face buried in the golden fur.

Soon, he approached. "They're calling the authorities. I'll need to bring them back here. I'll walk with you until we meet up with them."

As they approached the catwalk, voices reached them from up ahead. Soon, four Santa Rosa County personnel came into view. Kris bid Tony farewell with a boulder-size knot in her stomach. Whether from being forced to spend the day with him or capping it off with the grisly find in the forest, she wasn't sure. Probably both.

As a detective, maybe Tony was used to dealing with dead bodies. She wasn't.

Thunder rumbled again, closer than before.

"Come on, Bella." She picked up her pace to a jog, determined to reach her car before the rain moved in.

She didn't make it. Five minutes later, the sky opened up. Shortly after that, she loaded a sopping wet dog and her own dripping self into her red CR-V. She pulled her phone from her pack and called her best friend, hoping to cancel dinner plans. "I'm finished. Have you started cooking yet?"

"The casserole's in the oven, waiting for you to arrive."

She'd been afraid of that. "I need to borrow some dry clothes."

"Sure thing. We're getting the same storm. Maybe it'll pass before you leave here."

Kris ended the call and heaved a sigh. Forty minutes to Fort Walton Beach and an hour home, when she longed to head straight to Pensacola, pick up Gavin from the babysitter and spend the evening locked in her house, loving on her little boy and her dog.

But she couldn't let down her best-ever friend. Shannon and her boyfriend had broken up last night, and tonight she needed company. During the darkest period of Kris's life, Shannon had been there for her. Kassie had tried, but Kris had always felt closer to her best friend than either of her sisters.

When she pulled into Shannon's driveway, the rain was still coming down in sheets. She grabbed her umbrella and, after letting Bella out, made a dash for Shannon's front porch. Once there, Bella shook the water from her fur, showering Kris.

"Really?"

Moments after she rang the bell, the door swung open, and music spilled from the house. The smile Shannon wore held a lot of sympathy. "Come in. Here are some dry clothes." She handed Kris a T-shirt and yoga pants.

"I'll put Bella in the garage. Otherwise, your place will smell like wet dog."

"Go get changed. I've got Bella." Her voice was raised to compete with what poured from the sound system. She loved her music. Any time a popular band performed within a hundred-mile radius of Fort Walton Beach, she was likely in the audience.

As Kris headed down the hall, Shannon's voice followed her. "Come on, sweetie."

The smile she'd worn upon greeting her was a good sign. So was the lack of red, puffy eyes. She was handling the breakup well. Of course, Shannon always handled breakups well. She'd had enough practice. She threw off boyfriends like Kris cast off hand-me-down clothes.

When Kris walked into the kitchen, Shannon was throwing away an empty dog food can.

"You fed her. Thanks." Her friend didn't

have a dog, but Kris kept a stash of food there.

"I even toweled her off." She removed a casserole dish from the oven and placed it on a potholder in the center of the table. "Cheesy ground beef, the cheater's version of lasagna. Have at it."

Kris spooned a good-size serving onto her plate. "It smells fantastic."

Shannon sat opposite her. "Did you find your camper lady?"

"No. About forty of us were looking, a bunch of dogs, too, but there was no sign of her."

"That doesn't sound good."

"It gets worse. Tony and I discovered a body."

Shannon's eyes rounded. "Like a dead person?"

"Yep."

"Not the camper."

"No. He said the body had been there longer than that."

Shannon took a swig of iced tea. "Who

is this Tony person? Someone good-looking and eligible, I hope."

"Definitely good-looking." As much as she hated to acknowledge it.

"And eligible?"

"I don't know." He hadn't been wearing a ring. Not that she'd specifically looked for one. He'd held his sandwich in his left hand, and she hadn't been able to help but notice.

Shannon laid down her fork with a sigh. "What do you mean, you don't know? Girl, you need to ask these kinds of questions."

"Why, when I couldn't care less about the answers?"

Shannon shook her head in that *what-am-I-going-to-do-with-you?* way.

"I did get his full name."

"That's a start."

"Tony Sanderson."

Shannon's mouth fell open and snapped shut again. "Oh, *that* Tony."

"Yeah. Another reason to add to my

usual one for why I don't care whether he's available or not."

Shannon shook her head. "I'm so sorry. I should never have conned you into writing that note. I thought if he knew how you felt about him, he'd see y'all were meant to be more than just friends. I had no idea he'd use the note as a weapon."

She shrugged. "It's not like it permanently scarred me. You know, the whole sticks-and-stones thing." Except that whoever said words couldn't hurt apparently lived under a rock.

Kris scooped another bite of the noodle-beef-cheese mixture onto her fork. "Enough about Tony. How are *you* doing?"

"I'm all right. It was time." Shannon's gaze dipped to her plate, and she played with her food for several seconds, spearing and twirling it on her fork. Finally, she met Kris's gaze. "Carl was starting to scare me. He has anger issues."

Kris frowned. "Any chance he'll come back and try to hurt you?"

"I don't know." She squared her shoulders and lifted her chin. "But I say we banish both Tony and Carl from the rest of our conversation tonight. Let's plan another trip on the water."

"Already?" She and Shannon, along with Bella and Gavin, had spent the past weekend on Shannon's small cabin cruiser.

"It'll do us both good." Shannon spooned a bite into her mouth. "I wonder who the cute guy was that we passed on the water."

"We passed several cute guys on the water."

"The one we came up on early Sunday morning, with the cutoff jean shorts and no shirt."

Oh, yeah, him. They'd heard a splash ahead of them. As they'd approached, their engine on low, he'd been standing with his back to them, working over the side of the boat. Then he'd whirled, an anchor line or maybe cast net in his hand. "He didn't look thrilled to see us."

"We were scaring away his fish."

"Or maybe it was because you were shining your flashlight in his face."

"It wasn't in his face the whole time. Most of the time I had it aimed at his chest and abs. Very muscular ones, I might add."

Kris shook her head. Granted, the guy looked like he lived at the gym, but she wasn't nearly as swayed by good looks as her friend was.

"I should have asked if he was single, except I wasn't until last night." Shannon released a wistful sigh. "Maybe if I hang out at the public boat ramps, I'll run into him again."

"Shannon!"

"What?"

"You just got out of one relationship, and you're already trying to jump into another one."

"That's the best way to recover. If the horse throws you, get back in the saddle." Her tone grew serious. "It's like I've been telling you. No one will ever *replace* Mark, but isn't it time to get back out there? I mean, how long has it been since the accident, sixteen months?"

"Eighteen." Plus one week and two days.

"A year and a half. If Mark could talk to you right now, he'd say he doesn't want you pining away for him. He'd want you to be happy."

"I *am* happy." Relatively speaking.

She stood to take their plates and silverware to the dishwasher. Shannon followed with the casserole dish. By the time she'd put away the leftovers and cleaned the dish, Kris had finished wiping the counters.

She hung the dishcloth on the oven door handle. "Would you be disappointed if I ate and split?"

"Maybe a little, but I understand. After the day you've had, you're probably wiped."

She gave her a tired smile. "Wiped doesn't begin to describe it."

Kris walked from the kitchen. "I need to use your restroom before I leave." Then she'd get Bella and be on her way.

She stepped into the small room and hit the double switch, turning on the light and the exhaust fan. A minute later, the ring of the doorbell barely penetrated the rumble of the fan motor.

Her stomach tightened. *Carl.* Who else would it be at eight thirty at night, in weather like this? Hopefully the breakup hadn't ticked him off too badly.

"Don't answer it."

Shannon probably wouldn't hear her shouted words over the music, but she should have the sense to keep a locked door between herself and a possibly irate ex-boyfriend.

Kris stood and flushed the toilet. Washed and dried her hands. Opened the door. Shut off the light and exhaust fan.

The hair on her arms stood on end. Something wasn't right. If Shannon had opened the door, there would be arguing. If she'd kept it closed and locked, there'd be pounding and demands that she open it. But all was quiet except the music.

She tiptoed down the hall to the driving beat of Crossfade's "Cold" and stepped into the living room. Nothing was amiss. The wall to her left blocked the view of the kitchen. She moved forward, and the wall ended, opening the living room to the kitchen/dining area.

Blood *whooshed* through her ears, and her knees started to buckle.

A man stood between the table and the cabinetry, his back to her, a knife gripped in one latex-covered hand, his other stuffed into the pocket of his jeans. Shannon lay at his feet in an expanding pool of blood, hands clutching her stomach and chest, one leg slowly bending and straightening.

Kris pressed a hand to her mouth to stop the scream rising in her throat. But the gasp had already escaped. The intruder turned. It wasn't Carl. It was the boater she and Shannon had met early Sunday morning.

As he leaped toward her, his foot slid backward on the tile, slick with Shannon's blood, and he landed hard on that knee. Kris bolted across the living room. By the time she threw the deadbolt and opened the door, heavy footsteps pounded behind her.

She flew down the porch stairs. Cold rain poured down on her, drenching her for the second time.

She looked frantically around. There was no one to help her, no traffic in either direction. She ran for the side of the house. The intruder shot outside the same moment she rounded the corner. Had he seen her? If so, he'd be on her in moments. Her best option was to hide.

She climbed over the viburnum hedge that lined the side of Shannon's house and lay flat against the stucco wall. The hedge was thick, the branches of each shrub intertwining with the limbs of the next. If he wasn't looking, he'd never see her.

Heavy footsteps moved closer. As she peered between two of the shrubs, sneakers passed within feet of her face. She held her breath, heart pounding so hard it hurt. *Keep going.* Once he left the yard, she could make a run for a neighbor's house and have them call the police.

A rustle sounded nearby, then another

and another, each closer than the last. Her heart almost stopped. He was searching the hedge for her.

She low-crawled away from him, keeping her side pressed against the house. When she reached the front corner, she sprang to her feet and sprinted toward the road. A vehicle approached from her left. Her heart leaped into her throat. If she ran into the street in front of him, maybe he'd stop and help her.

The killer's footsteps pounded closer. By the time she reached the edge of the road, she could hear his labored breaths. A hand brushed her back.

She ran into the street. The headlights shining through the downpour were closer than she'd expected. The driver hadn't seen her. He'd never get stopped in time.

She made a desperate lunge, steeling herself for the sickening thud of metal against flesh. And the searing pain that would follow.

If she survived at all.

* * *

Tony jammed on his brakes, sending the Tundra into a skid. A sickening thud reverberated through the cab. A body rolled across his hood, slammed into his windshield and fell to the pavement.

Two figures had appeared out of nowhere. In the dark and pouring rain, he hadn't seen them until they'd been right in front of him. The larger one was lying in the road next to him. He wasn't sure about the smaller one. If he'd missed her, it hadn't been by much. He unfastened his seat belt and turned on his flashers. Before he could open the door, the man beside him rose and took off at a limping run.

Tony stepped from the truck. The man was headed down the property line between two houses. The smaller figure was running down the street toward his parents' place. That was where he was supposed to be.

He charged after the larger one. Someone didn't run after being struck by a car without good reason. Maybe they'd both committed a crime. Or maybe the man had been chasing the smaller person, who'd been trying to escape.

By the time he reached the backyards, he'd already lost sight of the man. For the next ten minutes, he darted from yard to yard, periodically stopping to listen for signs of movement. Finally, he had to admit defeat. In daylight, the injured man would never have escaped him. In the dark and pouring rain, visibility was too limited.

He jogged back toward his Tundra. The rain was slackening. As he neared the street, music flowed into the rainy night from one of the homes. It had barely registered when he'd stepped from his truck.

He continued forward. The yellow glow of his emergency flashers pulsed through the rain. The two people had apparently run out of the house that lay beyond. The front door was open, and light shone from beyond that first room.

He knew the woman who lived there. A friend had dated her briefly in high

school. That had been before his family
had moved from Pensacola to Fort Walton Beach at the end of his senior year.
Her parents had done the same two years
later, buying a house on the same street.
Was she the smaller figure he'd almost
hit? He couldn't say. Everything had happened too fast.

He approached his truck, which waited
just outside the glow of a nearby street-
light. Two feet away, he skidded to a stop.
A soft, shifting light came from inside the
cab. Someone was in his truck, possibly
with a cell phone. Maybe his. He'd left it
sitting in the cup holder after letting his
mom know he was on his way.

He approached slowly and drew his
weapon. If the man had doubled back and
was waiting for him inside the truck, he
wouldn't be caught off-guard. He stepped
closer. Definitely the glow of a cell phone.
Someone sat on his passenger floorboard,
head lowered, legs curled beneath them.
The figure didn't belong to a man.

He holstered his weapon. She posed no

threat. She held the phone in one hand and touched the screen with the other. She was shaking so badly, whatever she keyed in likely didn't resemble her brain's commands.

He hesitated. If she was the person he'd almost hit, and she'd been fleeing for her life, he didn't want to terrify her further.

He tapped on the window. She dropped the phone and scrambled onto the passenger seat, fumbling for the door handle. When he swung open the driver door, light flooded the interior of the cab. "It's okay. I'm a police officer. I can help you."

Her head swiveled toward him, and her eyes widened. His did, too.

Kris? She should have been back home in Pensacola. What was she doing hiding in his truck, a dripping, quivering mess?

He hurried around to the passenger side. When he opened the door, she looked up at him, her face streaked with tears, her short, dark hair plastered to her head. He reached into the truck to put a comforting hand on her shoulder. "Tell me what happened."

"Boater…knife…blood…everywhere." She was hyperventilating, gasping after every word. She ended the jumbled sentence with a sob.

He glanced behind him. "Where is Shannon?" She still lived there. The last he'd heard, her parents had let her assume the mortgage while they'd moved on. Taking cover inside would be safer than sitting outside with the man he'd hit on the loose.

"He stabbed her."

"Who stabbed her?"

"The boater." Another sob shook her shoulders.

"Did you call 911?"

"I tried."

That was what she'd been trying to do when he'd first seen her. He retrieved his phone from the passenger floorboard and made the call. When finished, he bent over to bring himself eye-to-eye with her. "They're sending police and ambulance. Is Shannon inside?"

Kris nodded.

"I'm going to check on her. Okay?" Maybe she was still alive. An ambulance would arrive within five or six minutes, but in situations like this, seconds counted.

She grasped his free hand. "Don't leave me."

"I won't, but you need to come up to the house with me."

"No, no, no." She shook her head so violently she sprayed him with rainwater.

"You don't have to come inside. Just wait on the porch."

She drew in a stabilizing breath. "Okay."

He helped her from the truck. She and Shannon Jacobs had been friends all through school, a friendship they'd obviously maintained. Though he didn't have the details, something horrific had happened here tonight.

She ascended the three steps and stopped at the open door, eyes averted so she couldn't see inside. "Please let Bella out."

"Where is she?"

"The garage."

"Give me a minute to check on Shannon."

"Okay. My purse is in there, too."

He nodded. That was why she didn't have her own cell phone or the means to drive away to safety.

When he stepped into the living room, his position offered him an angled view of the dining area. Two legs were visible around the living room wall, from the calves down. One foot was clad in a sandal, the other bare, its covering likely lost in the scuffle. The driving beat of a song he didn't know rammed into him, pounding in his chest. Ignoring it, he moved toward the kitchen.

Shannon lay faceup next to the kitchen table, blood pooling around her torso. One arm was bent, that hand resting on her abdomen. The other was extended at an angle from her body, palm up, fingers curled. Drying blood coated the underside of her hand and forearm.

His heart twisted. He dealt with violence on a regular basis. None of the cases were easy, but they were especially difficult when he knew the victims.

Careful to not disturb the scene, he squatted to press two fingers to her carotid artery. Nothing.

He rose and looked around the room. A purse hung over one of the chairs. If there'd been a struggle, nothing in the kitchen revealed it. The counters were spotless, bare except for a canister set and toaster oven. The only items occupying the table were a centerpiece, a napkin holder, and salt and pepper shakers.

He opened the door off the side of the kitchen. Bella wandered into the room and sniffed him.

"Hey, Bella. Let's go see your mommy." If the purse belonged to Kris, he'd let the crime scene people bring it out when they arrived.

As he walked back to the living room with the golden retriever in tow, sirens sounded in the distance. Kris was standing on the porch gripping the side railing.

Her gaze snapped up to meet his. "Shannon, is she…"

He nodded. "I'm so sorry."

The dog rushed to her, and she squatted to bury her face in the blond fur. Her shoulders shook with silent sobs. Tony wished he could be the one providing her comfort. At one time, he would have been. Then something had happened, something she was still holding against him, based on her coolness toward him this morning.

The first hour, the tension between them had been thick before she'd finally relaxed into her job. She'd had a crush on him throughout their junior and senior years, and the entire school had known about it before he had.

Their fathers had parted ways on unpleasant terms, too, at least on the Ashbaugh side. Not Jerry Sanderson. The man lived out his faith everywhere he went. It was an example Tony still tried to follow.

He cleared his throat, and she looked up at him, her face streaked with tears.

His chest tightened. "Do you think Bella would be able to pick up the killer's scent?"

"Possibly." She swiped her hands across both cheeks. "It's worth a try."

The first police car arrived a minute later, followed by an ambulance. Two officers stepped from the cruiser, and Tony approached the driver. He knew him from his years with Fort Walton Beach. "Parker, good to see you again." He nodded at the partner.

After returning the greeting, Bradley Parker looked toward the house, where Kris waited on the porch. "When we were dispatched, they weren't sure what kind of call it was."

"When I called it in, I wasn't sure myself. Turns out it's a homicide. The lady that lives here sustained multiple stab wounds."

Parker looked at his partner. "We need the CSI people out here." He brought his attention back to Tony. "And we'll put out an APB for the suspect."

"He left on foot." Tony glanced at Kris.

"The lady on the porch was here when it happened or got here right afterward. The guy went after her, and she ran. She can probably give a good description." He moved toward the porch, and Parker followed.

"I can tell you what he looked like." Kris had obviously been listening. "He was five ten or five eleven, well-built, with blond hair. It was long for a guy, touched his shoulders."

Parker made notes in the pad he'd taken from his pocket. "Facial hair?"

"Goatee and mustache, closely cut."

"Tattoos?"

"None that I saw."

After Parker radioed in the description, Tony motioned toward Bella. "Her dog is trained in search and rescue. I'd like to see if they can track him, in case he's still in the area."

"That's good. I'll go with you." He turned to his partner. "Stay here. Meet with the detectives and crime scene folks if they arrive before we get back."

Tony pointed out the path he'd seen the suspect take. Bella moved forward sniffing the air, and Tony followed Kris and her dog.

Parker fell in next to him. "Isn't the rain going to affect her ability to pick up the trail?"

Kris cast him a glance over her shoulder. "Golden retrievers are air scent dogs, so bad weather doesn't limit their ability."

"That's good." Parker lowered his voice. "How are you involved?"

"She ran out in front of me." He also kept his volume low to avoid distracting the woman and dog working in front of them. "I missed her but hit the guy pursuing her."

"Where is he?"

"He took off, and I lost him. It was dark and pouring rain."

He shifted his attention to Bella. She was working off-leash, Kris following at a slow jog. The dog's demeanor was different from when they'd performed their search in the woods. Her movements held excitement, as if she'd picked up on what her human wanted and was sure the prize was just ahead.

Bella led them between two other adjoining yards before turning to trot along the edge of the road. Suddenly, she stopped and retraced several steps. After walking in a couple of circles, sniffing the air, she sat.

Kris sighed. "She lost the scent. The killer probably got into a vehicle here."

As they headed back toward Shannon's house, Parker introduced himself to Kris and engaged her in conversation that centered around Bella. He loved dogs and seemed fascinated with Bella's abilities. Or maybe he was trying to put Kris at ease. If so, he was succeeding.

When they got back to Shannon's, the CSI people hadn't arrived yet. Kris leaned against her car, and Parker approached. "Do you mind answering a few questions?"

"Not at all."

He pulled a notepad from his pocket. "What happened here tonight?"

"I had dinner with my friend Shannon. I went to use the bathroom before leaving, and when I came out, she was on the floor bleeding. A man was standing over her with a knife."

"Did you hear anything before you came out?"

"Between the bathroom's exhaust fan and the music playing, I barely heard the doorbell. The guy took off after me but slipped in Shannon's blood and fell. That gave me a chance to get out."

"Do you know who he was?"

"Shannon and I met him while we were boating this past weekend."

"Do you have a name?"

"Just a first. Joe. It was early Sunday morning, shortly before daylight. We were in Choctawhatchee Bay, had lines out behind us and were trolling. We heard a big splash, figured someone had dropped anchor. Shannon shined her flashlight in that direction, and a boat was there."

"Do you know what kind?"

"An older Sea-Pro, white with blue trim, twenty-one foot, a one-hundred-fifty-horse Yamaha on the back."

Parker lifted his brows. "Those are some impressive details."

"My dad owns—owned a charter business. I know boats."

"I don't suppose you noticed the registration numbers."

She gave him a half smile. "I'm good but not that good."

"That's where this Joe was?"

"Yeah. He was standing with his back to us, leaning over the side holding a rope or something. He turned around, still holding it in one hand, and lifted the other to shield his eyes from Shannon's flashlight."

"What happened then?"

"I jumped on him for sitting there without at least a stern light. We could have hit him. He said the bulb had burned out."

"Any other conversation?"

"After Shannon asked and he told us his name, she swung the flashlight around to introduce the two of us. Shannon's always been super friendly."

Parker frowned. "First names or last names, too?"

"First names."

"Anything else?"

"I think that's it. We motored away."

After several more questions, Parker took down Kris's contact information. "The detectives will want you to do a composite and will probably ask you to try to point out where you saw the boater. That splash you heard probably wasn't an anchor. They'll want your friend's phone, too. Do you know where it is?"

"On the kitchen counter. She was cooking when I called her with my ETA. I noticed it when I got there."

Tony shook his head. "It wasn't there when I went inside."

"It had to be. It's beside—" Her eyes widened. "He took it."

"What do you mean?" Parker asked.

"The killer. I told you he was standing over Shannon holding a knife. His other hand was in his pocket. I'm guessing he'd just swiped Shannon's phone."

Lead filled Tony's gut. "That's not good."

"Why?"

As soon as she'd asked the question, her jaw went slack. "He took Shannon's phone, hoping it would help him locate Shannon's friends."

Tony nodded, that lead weight expanding into a boulder.

"One friend in particular."

TWO

Kris sat in a well-lit room at the Fort Walton Beach Police Department, the only sounds the soft strokes of a charcoal pencil against sketch paper.

The woman sitting across from her had introduced herself as Monica. She had a soothing voice, gentle smile and relaxed manner that put people at ease. Once assured that Kris was comfortable, she asked basic questions first—shape of the face, hair texture and length, absence or presence of facial hair and other broad characteristics.

Now, after rounding out the face slightly, making the eyes deeper set and squaring up the jaw, she was completing the finishing touches.

Finally, she laid the pencil down and turned the sketch pad around. "How is that?"

"Perfect." A shudder shook her shoulders. Maybe a little too perfect.

She could have come up with a decent composite just with what she'd seen in the glow of Shannon's flashlight. But the image of him standing over her friend's body, and the coldness in his eyes when they met hers, would remain with her the rest of her life. Last night, that image had haunted her dreams. With time, it would fade. It would have to, or she'd die from sheer exhaustion.

Monica thanked her, and Kris rose. "Thank *you*. It's pretty amazing how you can take something from someone's mind and transfer it to paper."

Monica rose, too, and shook her hand. "You made it easy."

Kris walked from the building and made her way toward her car. It had been a long day, one that had started with a trip on the water. She'd led the detectives to the location, or what she believed was the location, the best she could. She was confident she'd gotten close. Her sense of direction was good, but she knew the waters around Pensacola much better than those around Fort Walton Beach.

She pressed the key fob, and the locks clicked. At least she had nowhere else to go but home, once she picked up Gavin from the babysitter. Tomorrow, she needed to get back to the charter office. This morning, she'd managed to return some phone calls from yesterday that had been forwarded to her cell phone and had gotten a couple of charters scheduled. But after spending Tuesday on the search and rescue mission and being tied up in Fort Walton Beach all day today, her work was probably piling up. They'd hired a part-time accounting person, and Kris and Kassie traded off with helping Buck, their captain, with charters, but Kris tried to make it into the office three or four half days each week.

She settled into the driver's seat and

pulled her phone from her purse. She'd promised to text Kassie when she was on her way back to Pensacola.

Kris had called her after getting home last night, even though it had been late. The sleepiness in her sister's voice had fled instantly when Kris told her what had happened. She'd even offered to cancel the appointments she had at her salon today and accompany her to Fort Walton Beach. Kris had told her it wasn't necessary, but the offer had meant a lot.

There had been so much competition between them as children, which had continued as friction well into adulthood. In recent weeks, the friction had lessened, and the arguments had grown less frequent.

She wasn't holding her breath, though, thinking everything would be perfect from this point forward. She was too pragmatic. Unrealistic expectations only led to disappointment.

Before putting her phone away, she shot off a second text, this one to Tony. She'd rather not have any more contact with him. But last night, he'd insisted that she save his name and number and call him if she needed anything. He'd then amended those instructions to include keeping him posted on everything related to Shannon's death and any threats to herself. He'd made it clear that he expected a text before she left Fort Walton Beach. She'd reluctantly agreed.

He hadn't even wanted her to return to her home. She'd argued that she lived an hour away, and the killer had no idea where to find her, that it had taken him almost two days to find Shannon. He'd argued that her car had been sitting in Shannon's driveway the night she was killed. She'd responded that people couldn't look up owner information with a tag number, that it wasn't public information, and he'd insisted that didn't rule out the possibility. She'd reminded him that the killer had rung the bell, and Shannon had let him in, and she wouldn't do anything that careless.

The argument hadn't ended until she'd

agreed to look at her options, which would take time. Until then, she'd be as safe locked inside her house with the alarm and her dog as she'd be anywhere else.

Maybe she was putting more confidence in Bella's abilities than she should. After all, she was trained in search and rescue rather than taking down bad guys, like her future brother-in-law's dog, Justice. But she was super protective of both her people and would likely tear up anyone who tried to harm them.

After pressing the send icon, she dropped her phone into her purse and pulled out from the parking lot. Soon she was on Beal Parkway headed toward US 98, which would take her all the way to Pensacola. Ahead of her, a car sat on one of the side streets, waiting to pull onto Beal.

She glanced in her rearview mirror. Right now, Fort Walton Beach was the most dangerous place she could be, and she wouldn't risk picking up a tail and leading someone to her home.

In the second she'd checked her mirror,

the car she'd noticed earlier had started to shoot out in front of her. With a gasp, she jammed the brake. Her purse flew forward, making a somersault before landing on its side on the floorboard, contents strewn around it. She pressed the horn long and hard instead of calling the rude driver names.

After turning onto 98, she left Fort Walton Beach and drove through Mary Esther. On the long stretch that followed, traffic was moderate. Vehicles traveled in small clumps with large gaps between.

When she came upon a pickup pulling a landscape trailer, she moved into the left-hand lane. The burgundy SUV some distance behind her did, too. So did an older white pickup truck behind it.

As soon as she swung back into the right lane, the SUV sped past her, a middle-aged woman at the wheel. The pickup remained in the left lane, not traveling much faster than the landscaper. Maybe that was his normal traveling speed, considering the age of his truck. Or maybe he was staying at a distance so she couldn't identify him.

As the gap between them increased, some of the tension leached from her shoulders. She increased her speed some more. The truck didn't.

She released a sigh, the last of the tension fleeing. In less than thirty minutes, she'd be loading Gavin into his car seat and heading for home. At just after four, it wouldn't be time for dinner, but she'd start preparing it. They'd eat at five, watch a movie of Gavin's choice, likely involving a princess or superhero, and then go to bed early.

When she looked at the rearview mirror again, her heart leaped into her throat. The truck had sped up and was rapidly bearing down on her.

She glanced around her, her mistake immediately obvious. No other vehicles traveled with her. She was in one of those gaps she'd thought about earlier, alone with her pursuer. Trees lined both sides of the road, a grass median in the center.

She floored the accelerator and watched the speedometer climb. Seventy…seventy-five…eighty. Still the truck advanced. The speed limit here was fifty-five. At twenty-five miles an hour over, she should attract the attention of a cop. If there were any cops around. There weren't.

The pickup truck roared up next to her, engine wide open. She glanced at the driver. Although he'd hidden his long hair under a bandana, she had no doubt. She was looking at the boater.

She slammed on her brakes the same moment he swerved to the right. His rear bumper almost clipped the front of her car. He slid off the right shoulder, taking out a section of guardrail, and bounced back on, brakes depressed.

She mashed the accelerator and whipped around him in the left lane, making frequent glances in her rearview mirror. For several seconds, he weaved, trying to regain control of his truck. Soon he was speeding toward her again.

She squeezed the wheel until her hands

ached. Other vehicles traveled some distance ahead, a semitruck in their midst.
She just had to reach them before the
pickup caught up with her.

As he closed the gap between them, she
moved over to straddle the broken line
separating the two lanes. For the next minute or two, she held that position, moving
right when he tried to squeeze around her
on the shoulder and left when he tried to
squeeze around her on that side, all the
while hoping he didn't have a gun. She
needed to call for help, but her phone was
somewhere on the floorboard, along with
the rest of the contents of her purse.

Ahead of her, two vehicles moved into
the left lane to pass the tractor trailer. She
backed off the accelerator slightly. If she
timed it correctly, as soon as she reached
the other vehicles, she could pull up next
to the semi and match its speed until she
figured out what to do.

As she got closer, a blue Pontiac approached the semitruck in the right lane. It
was the only vehicle that hadn't yet passed.

She backed off the accelerator some more, eyes on the Pontiac. *Stay where you are.* A few more seconds and she'd swing all the way into the left lane, ready to travel next to the trailer.

The car's left signal came on. "No!" She hit the brakes, and the pickup truck moved to the right. The driver started to change lanes, then jerked back fully into his own.

Kris breathed a sigh of relief and was traveling next to the trailer seconds later. The pickup was right behind her, about three car lengths back. There was nothing he could do to her now, with her somewhat protected by the truck. If he had a gun, he'd have already shot her.

The speed limit reduced as she passed into Wynnehaven Beach. If the traffic co-operated, she'd keep her position next to the semi. Retrieving her phone from the floorboard while stopped at a red light wasn't going to happen—there weren't any traffic signals along this stretch of highway.

Soon she left the small town behind. The

speed limit increased to fifty-five, and trees again lined both sides of the road. Each mile was taking her closer to Pensacola, leading a killer straight to her home. She needed a plan.

Another small town lay just ahead—Navarre. As she drew closer, her pulse picked up speed. Her idea just might work.

She drew up even with the cab of the semi. In the distance, 87 veered off to the right, with a long, gentle exit lane. If she timed it right, she could whip off 98 and onto 87. By the time the driver of the truck knew what she'd done, he'd be well past the exit.

She eased past the semi, staying in the left lane. The pickup crept forward, too. Ahead, a double white sign showed 98 West continuing straight ahead, 87 North to the right.

She waited to make her move, gripping the wheel, jaw tight, back straight. The exit lane began, but she couldn't act yet. She had to wait until the road started to split.

Now! She floored the accelerator and turned the wheel to the right, crossing in front of the semi and onto 87, missing the truck's front bumper by less than twenty feet.

A horn sounded behind her, long and loud and angry. She cringed and waved. "Sorry." The driver would understand if he knew her situation.

There was no way the pickup could have followed, but she checked her rearview mirror anyway. Another vehicle was making its way off 98, a little silver car.

She continued around the long, gentle curve. The ordeal wasn't over yet. The Chevy pickup driver would take the next road and double back to look for her. She had to find somewhere to hide. Then she could retrieve her phone and call 911.

She needed to get away from 87. It was the first place the killer would look for her. But she had no idea where to go. As many times as she'd been through Navarre going to and from Shannon's, she'd never strayed off 98.

She slowed to take the next right, Harrington Drive. A block ahead, a sign announced Santa Rosa County Library. She turned into the parking lot and slid into a space next to a cargo van.

Once she'd shifted into Park and killed the engine, she ran around to the passenger's side to move her purse and retrieve her phone from the pens, receipts and other items littering her floor. Then she stood at the front of her car and made the call she'd been dying to make for the past thirty minutes. Her red CR-V wasn't visible from Harrington. But she wasn't taking any chances. She'd remain poised and ready to run into the library at the first sign of a white pickup truck.

There would be no relaxing evening at home tonight. She needed to come up with a plan. Even without the ability to get into DMV records, it would just be a matter of time until the killer found her. He'd probably start with Navarre and the surrounding communities and expand outward from there. Eventually his search would lead him to Pensacola.

Right to her and Bella and Gavin's doorstep.

Tony had been right. She needed to find another place to live.

And she needed to do it fast.

Tony stepped from the police station into the heat and humidity of an August afternoon. Judging from the few puffy white clouds in the sky, they weren't going to get a repeat of last night's storms.

He'd started the day attending a briefing. One of the discussion items had been Shannon's murder. Though it had happened in Okaloosa County and was in the jurisdiction of the Fort Walton Beach PD, the details of the case were being disseminated to all the surrounding agencies.

Last night's search had produced nothing—no prints, no evidence, no witnesses. Today, authorities had requested location information from Shannon's cell phone provider. Kris had also tried to point out the location where she and Shannon had come upon the boater and then helped the artist create a composite of the killer. If her memory for faces was as good as it was for boats, she'd make the ideal witness.

Tony climbed into the driver's seat of the black Chevy Tahoe, his department-assigned SUV. Since Kris had just texted him to say she was leaving Fort Walton Beach, he now had her number, too, had even saved it in his contacts.

He hoped she wouldn't mind him using it, because that was exactly what he intended to do. Granted, it wasn't his case, but he had a personal stake in it. He knew the victim, his parents lived a few doors down and now someone he cared about was in the killer's crosshairs.

He cranked the vehicle, and before he could back out, the ringtone on his phone sounded. He wouldn't have to call Kris. She'd beaten him to it.

He swiped to accept the call. "Hey, you."

"Hey."

It was just a single word, but it held a lot of tightness. Between their time together in the woods and their interaction last night, he'd thought they'd come to a truce.

Or maybe that was fear he heard. "Is everything all right?"

"Shannon's killer came after me."

"Where are you?" Wherever she was, he'd go to her. She could explain everything then.

"Navarre. I'm at the Santa Rosa County library. The police will be here any minute."

Good. She'd dialed 911 before calling him. "I'm on my way. Stay put until I get there."

Whatever had happened, he wouldn't let her drive home and walk into her house alone. Once they arrived, he'd thoroughly check everything. Then he'd make another attempt at trying to talk her into staying somewhere else.

He ended the call and headed in that direction. Navarre was only thirty-five minutes away. Slightly less if he hurried.

As soon as he turned off of Harrington, he scanned the library's parking lot. A Santa Rosa County sheriff cruiser sat in one of the parking spaces, but Kris's red CR-V wasn't there. Had she decided not to wait for him?

He continued his approach, drawing closer to a white cargo van that was almost too long for its space. Beyond it, a red bumper came into view. The van had enabled her to effectively hide from anyone who ventured past.

After pulling into a parking space, he got out and approached her car. She stood next to it, talking to a sheriff deputy. Another was inside the cruiser on his radio.

The first deputy nodded at him and turned his attention back to Kris. "Anything else you can tell me?"

"That's pretty much it. I figured this would be a good place to hide out while I called you guys."

Tony watched the deputy walk toward his vehicle. When he approached Kris, she gave him a weak smile. "I'm sorry to run you all the way out here, but I'm glad you came."

"What happened? I know you just relayed the whole thing to the deputy, but maybe you can give me the CliffsNotes version."

"When I was on one of those deserted, wooded stretches of 98, a pickup truck pulled up next to me and tried to run me off the road. It was the same guy who killed Shannon. I jammed on my brakes, and while he was trying to regain control of his truck, I sped past him then drove like a maniac until I was able to get next to a semi."

"How were you able to lose him?" In broad daylight, with good weather and rural surroundings, that had to have been quite a feat.

"Let's just say there's a pretty ticked-off truck driver on 98 right now. At least, there was as of about thirty minutes ago. I cut across in front of him to make an emergency exit onto 87. The killer couldn't get around the truck in time to follow me."

And then she'd hidden out at the library, concealed by a cargo van. She obviously thought quickly under pressure. Of course, she'd always been smart. If it hadn't been for their joint study sessions, he'd have probably failed high school chemistry.

"What kind of pickup was the guy driving?" The deputy would have asked that question, too. But he wanted to know for himself.

"A Chevy. I noticed the bow tie on the grill when he was behind me."

"Do you know what kind of Chevy?"

"A white one." She gave him a half smile. "I'm afraid I don't know trucks like I know boats. I do know it was older, though, maybe not an antique, but probably pretty close."

"During the brief time he was in front of you, you didn't happen to notice any part of the tag number, did you?"

"Uh-uh. I was too focused on trying to stay alive."

He put a hand on her shoulder and

squeezed it. "You did good." He dropped his hand. "Are you going home now?"

"Yes, after I pick up Gavin from the babysitter."

So she had a kid. Likely an ex-husband, too. Though they were the same age, his life was a lot less complicated. He'd fallen in love a couple of times but had come out of the experience without any attachments. They'd both been fine Christian women. One of the relationships, he'd ended. The other, the woman had. Both times, the decision had been somewhat mutual. Those women were now happily married, and there were no hard feelings on either side.

She opened the Honda's door and slid into the driver's seat.

He stepped closer. "I know I said this last night, but you need to get somewhere safe. You've been in danger since the moment you and Shannon heard this guy dumping whatever it was that he dumped. He has no idea what you might have seen. He already killed Shannon, and now he's coming after you. Except he'll be more determined. Not only is he afraid you witnessed whatever went down on the water, you can also identify him as Shannon's killer."

"I know. I've been thinking about it."

"Do you have a friend you can stay with, or maybe Kassie?"

"Someone I'd feel comfortable piling in on with a kid and a fairly large dog? That friend is dead."

Her tone held hardness. Bitterness seemed to have replaced the brokenness he'd seen last night. He hoped over time she'd see her way past it.

She heaved a sigh. "I don't want to put anyone else in danger—my friends or my sister."

"What about the space above Ashbaugh Charters? Is it still vacant?" It wasn't an ideal solution, especially if the killer discovered her maiden name, but it might be a safer option than home, depending on how secure her house was.

"No one is staying there, if that's what you mean. I wouldn't classify it as vacant. It's been used as extra storage space for years, so it's filled with dusty old boxes. Some critters have probably taken up residence there, too."

"How about if we go by on our way to your house? We can check it out together."

"Sounds good. But don't say I didn't warn you."

"I'll be prepared for the worst."

He walked to his vehicle and followed her from the parking lot. Twenty minutes later, they pulled into two of the parallel parking spaces lining Government Street. Located at the edge of the Seville Quarter, the New Orleans–style building housed the charter office and another space, each with a second story. Back when their fathers had been partners, her family had owned the entire building.

He stepped from his vehicle and met her on the sidewalk in front of a fifteen-paned French door. Above it, gold script on a one-by-three-foot sign spelled out Ashbaugh Charters. The other half of the building was vacant, as evidenced by the for-rent sign in the front window.

Tony nodded in that direction. "If the space above the charter office is uninhabitable, what about up there?"

"Kassie and I have it listed for rent. We'd have to change our ad. 'Space comes with a squatter already installed upstairs.'"

He gave her a playful poke in the side. "You can't be a squatter on your own property."

"I guess not. But I think I'd be much safer with an alarm. That space has been empty so long, it's not protected by a security system. The charter office has one."

"Monitored?"

"Yep. It's even got a motion sensor, which we'll have to disable if I'm going to stay there."

She unlocked the front door and swung it open. The squeal of the alarm began instantly. After punching in the code and locking them in, she walked to a wooden door in the back right corner of the lobby area.

"Follow me."

She swung open the door, revealing a narrow wooden staircase, and flipped the light switch next to it. "I haven't been up here in ages, so I have no idea what we'll find."

"We'll make the discovery together."

He followed her up the stairs. Dozens of dusty boxes filled the space, along with some old chairs, folding tables, a broken-down vacuum and what looked like boat parts. The most recent additions had been thrown in haphazardly, boxes not stacked, items left in the middle of the floor.

He surveyed the mess. "It's actually not as bad as I thought. Most of this stuff could be stacked against the wall."

"There's not even a bed up here."

"We can clean everything up and move one in."

She crossed her arms and leaned against a stack of boxes. "I keep hoping I'll wake up and realize this is all a bad dream, that Shannon will be calling any minute to make plans for our next get-together or tell me about her latest crush." Her gaze dipped to the floor. "I called her parents last night. I wanted them to hear it from me instead of the police. Her mom fell apart. She put Shannon's dad on. He handled it a little better than she did, but neither of them will ever get over this."

She looked up at him, her eyebrows drawn together. "You have to catch this guy."

"We're doing everything we can."

She looked around the room and heaved a sigh. "There's no way I can face this tonight, or even next week. Even with help."

"Don't worry about it now. We'll pick up your son. Then I'll follow you home. Once there, we'll figure out the safest place for you to be, and I'll make that happen."

She looked at him with raised brows. "When did you get so bossy?"

Without further argument, she bounded down the stairs in front of him. She was the same size she'd been in high school—slender, petite, obviously active. She'd been a runner then. If she still ran, recent events were going to curtail that activity for a while.

He reached the lobby and followed her to the door, where she pressed a button on the alarm panel to arm the system. A sense of protectiveness surged through him. Based on what he'd seen in his headlight beams last night, the man chasing her was at least a head taller than she was and probably double her weight. Left to face him alone, she wouldn't stand a chance.

He'd see to it that didn't happen. If he couldn't be with her himself, he'd make sure someone else was.

For the past ten years, he'd felt bad about how they'd parted at the end of high school. Throughout junior and senior high, he'd considered her one of his closest friends. Somehow, he'd hurt her without intending to. He'd always tried to follow the advice in Romans to live at peace with everyone, as much as he was able, but with their fathers parting ways, summer break rapidly approaching and his family moving to Fort Walton Beach, whatever had gone wrong between them had seemed to put a permanent wedge in their relationship. It was a loss he'd felt for a long time, one that was still there, ten years later.

Then yesterday, God had put her in his path, not once, but twice. Maybe this time he wouldn't blow it.

God, please give me a chance to make right what I messed up in the past.

THREE

Kris pulled into her driveway, Tony's department-assigned vehicle behind her. He'd followed her to the babysitter's house, where he'd waited in his vehicle.

While she helped Gavin from his car seat, he approached. As much as she'd rather deal with everything after a good night's sleep in her own bed, something told her the discussion about her living arrangements was nowhere near over.

She removed the straps from Gavin's shoulders and took his hand. When he'd climbed from the car, she picked him up. Tony was standing several feet away, watching her.

"This is my son, Gavin."

"Hello, Gavin. How are you?" Although

he greeted him, even offered him a small smile, he didn't step any closer. His back was rigid, his jaw tight.

Was he judging her—a single woman with a kid? The Sanderson family had always been über religious. Based on the things her father had told her, it had all been for show.

But Tony knew she was married, or had been. The day of the search for the missing camper, Teresa had introduced her as Kris Richards. He'd even asked about the name change. Apparently, he just didn't like kids.

She looked at her son. "This is Mr. Tony. He's a policeman like Uncle Jared. Can you say hi?"

Gavin raised his hand in a little wave, and Kris headed up the curved concrete walkway toward the front door. Blooming annuals lined the path on either side of her. Perennials formed a backdrop in varying shades of green, their spring blooms having shriveled and fallen off some time ago.

"You're still in the home where you grew up."

She looked at Tony over one shoulder. "Yeah, I moved back when…a year and a half ago. It was a good arrangement. Gavin and I didn't have to be alone, and Dad got good home-cooked meals. The only downside for him was that he couldn't drink around Gavin and me or even come home smelling of alcohol."

Her father's alcoholism wasn't any secret. Neither was her mother's desertion, taking off to the Bahamas with her boyfriend. Or the conflict between her and her sisters. Since their fathers were in business together and they'd developed a friendship of their own, Tony had had a front-row seat to the rotten Ashbaugh family dynamics.

The contrast between them and the picture-perfect Sandersons had been huge. The messed-up Ashbaughs had probably been a topic of conversation around the Sanderson dinner table more than once.

She stepped onto the front porch and

unlocked the door. After disarming the alarm, she invited him inside.

"You and your son live here alone now?"

So he knew the situation with her father. Another thing for the Sandersons to gloat over. Of course, if Tony had access to the internet, TV or a newspaper, he would have known. The entire story had been quite public—her father's disappearance and the charges when he'd shown back up.

She and her father had shared a special bond, and all her life, she'd made excuses for him. A few months ago, she'd finally taken off the blinders.

"Yes, it's just us and Bella."

As soon as she said the name, the golden retriever padded into the entry to greet them. As Kris closed and locked the door behind them, Tony knelt to pet the dog. He was far better with animals than kids.

He straightened and frowned at her. "You're definitely not safe here."

"I have an alarm." But it no longer brought the comfort it had before.

"This place is huge. There are too many ways in."

He was right about the size. The Victorian-style home right on Bayou Texar *was* huge. It had been in her family since her great-grandparents had had it built at the turn of the last century.

"If someone kicked in the door and triggered the alarm, how long do you think it would take the police to get here?"

"I don't know." A lot longer than it would take an intruder to run upstairs and kick in her bedroom door. Dread trickled through her, and she tightened her hold on her son.

He followed her to the kitchen, where she laid her purse on the counter and lowered Gavin to the floor. He looked up at Tony and then back at her before trotting off to the family room.

His little-boy voice drifted back to them. "I'm gonna pway wif my twuck."

Tony crossed his arms. "If you stay at the charter office, you'll be right downtown. The police would be there in a minute or two. Someone would have to be pretty desperate to break in the front door six feet from a well-lit, well-traveled road."

"The back door opens into a parking lot. It's much more deserted back there."

"Not as deserted as behind the house."

He was right again. The family room, dining room and downstairs bedroom all had double French doors overlooking the backyard and offering a view of the bayou beyond. Someone could break out a pane of glass in any of them and reach through to unlock the door. Or they could just kick the door in. Unfortunately, neither location felt safe.

She pressed her lips together. "No serious discussions on an empty stomach. I'm going to get some supper ready. Would you like to stay?" Maybe he'd say no. She was too tired to try to make polite conversation. But after everything he'd done for her in the past twenty-four hours, the least she could do was feed him.

"That sounds great."

"We'll be having leftovers." One more

opportunity for him to back out. When she'd fixed her and Gavin's dinner Monday night, she'd made extra, as she often did, planning to reheat it two nights later. If Tony wanted to stay, she could stretch it, especially if she added a salad and some bread.

"Hey, I'm a single guy. You'd be appalled at some of the things we eat and call dinner. Leftovers are fine. Do you need any help?"

"I've got dinner covered if you wouldn't mind taking Bella out." A neighbor had come over to walk her at lunchtime. "Her leash is hanging in the foyer by the front door."

Tony walked from the room, and she pulled two casserole dishes from the fridge, one holding chicken divan and the other cooked rice. After taking the chill off with the microwave, she put them into the oven on low and set to work making the salad.

She was almost done when Tony reappeared, Bella trotting after him. "Potty break complete. What else can I do?"

"You can make yourself at home."

Once she'd finished the salad, she sliced and buttered some Italian bread and sprinkled it with garlic. Soon a childish voice drifted to her from the front of the house.

"See my twuck?"

Uh-oh. Gavin was apparently trying to engage Tony in conversation. She'd better go rescue him—Tony, not her son.

When she walked into the living room, Tony was standing in front of the fireplace, holding a picture frame to his chest and looking down at Gavin.

"That's a nice dump truck. Did Mommy get it for you?"

"No. Aunt Kassie."

Kris stepped into the doorway and leaned against the jamb. "She got it for his second birthday a few months ago."

He placed the frame back on the mantle. It held a picture of Mark, one of her favorites. He was wearing his blue dress uniform, standing between two poles, one holding an American flag, the other the Air Force flag. The picture was taken right after he'd received the Air Force Achievement Medal.

Tony nodded toward the photo. "I take it that's Mr. Richards?"

"Yes, Mark."

His gaze went to the flag sitting in the center of the mantle, folded inside its triangular wood-and-glass display case. "I'm sorry for your loss."

"Thank you."

Several moments of awkward silence passed before she pushed herself away from the door jamb. "I'm going to go toast the garlic bread, and then dinner will be ready."

"How about if I set the table?"

"Sure."

She headed back to the kitchen with Tony and Gavin in tow.

Once the garlic bread was toasted, Tony helped her place everything on the table. "For leftovers, this looks great. It smells wonderful, too."

"Thanks. This is one of my favorite meals. Super easy to make, too."

When they'd all sat, Gavin folded his hands and looked at Tony. Mealtimes with Kassie and Jared always began with prayer. In Gavin's mind, company at the dinner table meant someone would be saying grace.

Instead of dishing up the food, Tony looked at her, waiting.

She dipped her chin. "Go ahead."

He offered a simple prayer for protection and ended with thanks for the food. Gavin echoed his "amen" with a hearty one of his own. Tony was probably impressed.

She should set the same example for Gavin that had been set for her. By her mother, anyway. Until she decided to take off.

She picked up her fork and stabbed a piece of cubed chicken. "I don't suppose you heard anything today about the missing camper."

"Not a thing."

"Or the woman we found in the woods?"

"Not yet. It'll take time to identify her."

"When we discovered her, you said 'not

again.'" She'd found the comment odd but had been too addled at the time to question it. "What did you mean?"

His gaze shifted to the side, and several seconds passed in silence. Finally, he spoke. "Three months ago, I worked a case where a woman disappeared from Milligan. Her car was abandoned at the edge of a wooded area along Route 90. She was found near Pensacola two days later." He cast a glance at Gavin before continuing. "Same shape as the woman we found."

Head smashed in with a blunt object, maybe a hammer. At two years old, Gavin likely wasn't tuning in to any of their conversation, but it was sweet of Tony to consider it. "The case you worked, the lady was dark-haired and slender, like our Julia Morris?"

He nodded, his expression grim. "That victim and now the woman we discovered. If we find that Julia Morris met the same end..."

She finished the thought for him. "You have a serial killer on your hands."

His gaze locked with hers. "Don't talk to anybody until the police are ready to make it public."

"I won't."

He opened his mouth as if to say something else, then stopped. But she didn't need him to voice the thought aloud. She could see it in his eyes.

"Dark hair, slender, physically fit. I match the profile. But so do countless other women." Maybe she was at risk, but the possibility was slim. The threat from the boater was much more real.

Throughout the rest of the meal, Tony stayed true to his promise to not force her to discuss her living arrangements. Once they'd each taken their last bite, though, that restraint ended.

"Are we in agreement that the charter office would be safer for you guys than here?"

"Probably."

"Do you have a better suggestion?"

"Mark's parents would be ideal. His father is a retired military man with a decent collection of guns. And he knows how to use them."

"Great. How about calling them now?"

"Not so fast. There are two problems. First, they live in Ohio, so I'd be leaving Kassie to handle the charter business alone, on top of her responsibilities with her salon. I'm afraid it would be too much for her."

"It would be temporary." Tony frowned. "If this guy has his way, you won't be around to help her with the business… ever. And someone else will be raising your son."

She suppressed a shudder. If Tony hadn't been headed to his parents' house at the moment she'd run into the street last night, and if there'd been no semitruck to aid in her escape from 98, she wouldn't be standing in her kitchen right now arguing about living arrangements.

"What's the other problem with staying with your in-laws?"

"They just left for a Mediterranean cruise and won't be back for two weeks."

He gave her a sharp nod. "So, if you do decide to stay with them, what are your intentions for the next two weeks?"

She pulled her lower lip between her teeth. The thought of staying in the huge old house alone terrified her. She'd thought she could do it. That had been before the second attempt on her life. "I'll move into the space over the charter office."

He expelled a breath, both his shoulders and his facial features relaxing. "Tonight?"

"Tomorrow. I'm too tired to even think of tackling it tonight."

"All right. I'll help you with the move. Meanwhile, I'm sleeping downstairs, either on one of your couches or in your guest room. I'll look around and decide which."

She cocked one eyebrow at him. "You really *have* gotten bossy."

Whatever argument she would have come up with a few hours ago didn't make it to her lips. In fact, it didn't even form in her thoughts.

She didn't want Tony with her. He taken that stupid note she'd written and mocked her with it. It had happened more than a decade ago, but she still wasn't ready to let it go.

Right now, though, none of that mattered. Because tonight, Tony was exactly what she needed—someone who would offer the comfort of his presence with no pressure for anything more.

Maybe eventually she would be able to once again think of him as a friend. But that would be all. Her heart still belonged to Mark. If she ever reached a point where she was ready to move on, it would have to be with a man who liked kids. That requirement was non-negotiable, because she and Gavin were a package deal.

Tony pulled out from the parking lot of Captain Joey Patti's Seafood Restaurant, a plastic bag in the seat beside him. It held two grilled mahi fish tacos and was currently filling the confines of his truck with mouthwatering aromas.

Once he got to his apartment, he'd call Kris and see what her schedule looked like. He hadn't talked to her since he'd dropped her off at the charter office that morning. She'd warned him then that she had a full day, with two back-to-back charters, as well as some paperwork to handle at the office.

Even though it was now five o'clock in the afternoon, her work wasn't over. His wasn't either. They both had a long evening ahead of them.

He was actually looking forward to it. Spending time with Kris was every bit as enjoyable now as it had been when they were in high school, maybe even more so. He could just about see something serious developing between them. She was smart, witty and ambitious. And she was beautiful. Falling for her would be so easy.

But he wouldn't do it. She had a kid, and he'd made a vow fourteen months ago. Never again would he be responsible for someone else's child.

He backtracked a short distance down

Garden Street to make his right turn onto Coyle. Palmilla Apartments was ahead and to the left. The recently built complex was large and upscale. His own apartment was tiny—just an efficiency—but it was nice. And it was plenty for a petless, childless single guy.

Once inside, he laid his bag on the small kitchen table, sank into a chair and dialed Kris's number. While waiting for the call to connect, he offered a brief prayer of thanks for the food. Her "hello" came right on the tail of his silent "amen."

He put her on speaker and pulled the Styrofoam container from the bag. "How is everything going?"

"Good. My charters went well. Kassie came in the last part of the day, and we tackled some of the mess upstairs."

"Wow, you guys are ambitious." She sounded a lot more energetic than last night.

"Don't get your hopes up too much. We hardly made a dent in it."

"No problem. We'll get as far as we can.

I've got the day off tomorrow, so whatever we don't get done tonight, we can finish in the morning."

"That'll work for me, too. I don't have anything till the afternoon."

He picked up the first taco. "Are you still at the charter office?"

"No, I rode home with Kassie. We're having dinner in a few minutes. What about you?"

"I got takeout from Captain Joey Patti's."

"Mmm, the best. Not to say that my sister isn't feeding me well."

"When you're done, how about if I take you to get whatever you guys will need over the next few days? Then we can go by the charter office."

They'd agreed last night that she shouldn't drive her car until this was over or she was able to leave town altogether. The killer knew what she drove, was confident enough in that fact to chase her down 98. No, that candy-apple-red CR-V needed to stay in her garage.

His phone vibrated, and an incoming call flashed across the top of the screen.

"I gotta go. My captain's calling."

He touched the screen with one pinkie to accept the call. "Hey, Keith. What's up?"

"I know you're done for today and are supposed to be off tomorrow, but we've had a new development."

"What kind of development?"

"Pictures. Quite a few of them."

"Of?"

"Slender women with dark hair."

Tony laid down his taco and sat up straighter.

His captain continued. "When you guessed we might have a serial killer on our hands, it looks like you might have hit the nail on the head."

"I want to see them. I'll be there in about ten minutes."

He ended the call and inhaled his last taco, leaving the pita chips and salsa for tomorrow. On the way down to his vehicle, he called Kris back. "I'll be a little later.

I've got to go back to the station. I'll call you when I'm done."

Six minutes after leaving his apartment complex, he was there. Palmilla's location was another one of the reasons he'd chosen it.

He hurried into the station and met Keith in his office. "So, what's the story?"

"Santa Rosa County got a call. A maid in a cheap hotel in Holley. She was cleaning the room of one of the guests. He'd only been there for three days, but she claimed that, the way he looked at her, he gave her the willies right from the get-go."

"That's where the pictures came from?"

"Yep. He had them in a dresser drawer and didn't have it closed tight. She got curious, pulled it open farther and recognized several pictures of Julia Morris lying on top."

"The missing camper."

"Yep. She'd seen the news story that aired last night, with the plea that anyone with any information come forward. She called 911 from her cell phone and hurried out of the room as the guy was pulling up. He took one look at her and shot out of there as if the whole county was in hot pursuit."

"Did the hotel clerk have any information? Name, address, vehicle description, tag number?"

"They got it all. It just wasn't any good. He gave a false ID, and the tag was stolen. The only thing they had was that he was driving a white Chevy pickup, older model."

Tony stiffened. Just the kind of truck Shannon's killer was in when he went after Kris. But that didn't mean much. White was the most popular color for pickup trucks. His Tundra was even white.

Keith continued. "The guy wrote '95 on the paperwork, but that detail may not be any more accurate than the others. Based on the description your lady friend gave yesterday, it was pretty close. If it's the same truck."

His captain handed him a stack of photos—the copies that Santa Rosa County had distributed to the other agencies. "We're going to keep an eye out and see if he returns to claim his possessions, but it's not likely. He didn't leave anything of value. Nothing that offered a clue to his identity, either."

Tony looked at what he held. The top photo resembled what they'd been given the day of the search. Definitely the missing camper. She was walking, almost in profile, a camera hanging from a strap around her neck, trees in the background. Leaves encroached on the edges of the photo and in the foreground, as if the one doing the photographing had taken advantage of the foliage to conceal himself.

He slid the photo to the back of the stack. The next several featured Morris also, all taken around the same time. The odds of finding her alive had gone down each day she'd been missing. With the find of the photos, they'd dropped to near zero. How long did the creep stalk his prey before moving in for the kill? Where had he disposed of her body?

A few photos later, the subject changed—the same dark hair, the same slight build, but different features. Tony's jaw tightened. "Amanda Driscoll."

This was probably the reason Keith had called him. Driscoll was the Milligan woman who'd been killed and had her body dumped near the outskirts of Pensacola. Like with Morris, there were a half dozen photos, obviously candid shots.

Tony didn't recognize the next subject. "Who is this?"

"Dawn Baucom."

"The name doesn't ring a bell."

"That's the woman you and your friend found in the woods on Monday. They just ID'd the body this afternoon."

Tony nodded. Three young women—two dead, one missing. Appearance a common thread between them. Now definitively connected.

He slid the next three photos under the stack, like he had the others.

A smiling face stared up at him, glowing with a natural beauty. Skin tanned to a healthy glow. Hair cut in a pixie, the short strands lying in soft layers. Dark eyes tugged at him, even from a photograph.

His chest tightened around a cold knot of dread. One more young woman connected to the others. One more target of a serial killer.

"That's the only woman we haven't yet identified." Keith's words sliced through his scattered thoughts. "You know her?"

He nodded. They hadn't identified her yet because she hadn't been reported missing or found dead.

But she'd been targeted. She'd landed in the killer's sights, and it would just be a matter of time.

Yes, he knew her.

He forced the response through a constricted throat.

"Her name is Kristina Ashbaugh-Richards."

FOUR

Kris pushed herself away from Kassie's dining room table.

"Dinner was delicious. Thanks for the invite."

Kassie always claimed that Kris was the gourmet cook of the family, but Kassie didn't do so badly herself.

Kris wiped remnants of baked chicken and scalloped potatoes from her little boy's face and hands. He didn't eat the green peas with nearly as much gusto as he had the rest of his dinner.

She pulled him from his high chair. "Go play while Mommy helps Aunt Kassie clean up the kitchen."

He ran from the room and disappeared down the hall, Bella following. A half minute later, the clatter of plastic and metal told her he'd dumped the toy bin in the spare bedroom.

Kris winced. "I should have told him to take out one toy at a time. Tony will be here any minute."

"Let him play. I'll pick up the toys after you guys leave."

Kris stacked their plates and laid the silverware across the top before heading to the sink. "When Tony showed up to help with the search efforts, I wasn't thrilled, even less so to be stuck working with him as my partner. But I have to admit, as much as I hated seeing him, I'm really lucky to have him hanging around right now."

Kassie frowned. "Luck has nothing to do with it."

Kris rolled her eyes. "I know, it's all about God."

She tried to tamp down the annoyance surging through her but wasn't quite successful. She'd liked her sister better before she'd gotten back into church and started thinking that God was the answer to everything.

Kassie rinsed the last of the plates Kris had brought over and put it in the dishwasher. "God is guiding your life, even if you don't see it now."

Kris swiped the sponge back and forth across the counter with more force than necessary. "He's guiding my life the same way He guided the pickup truck driver to cross the center line and hit Mark head on? The same way He guided Mom to take off and leave us behind? Thanks, but no thanks. I'll do without His guidance."

Kassie didn't respond. When Kris looked over at her, her eyes held sadness.

The annoyance instantly morphed to guilt. She shouldn't have snapped. Her sister's mini sermons were only because she cared.

Kris heaved a sigh. "I'm sorry. Things are tough right now, but I don't mean to take it out on you."

"It's all right." Kassie gave her a small smile. "You've been through a lot, and the recent events aren't helping any." Her smile faded. "Are you okay with seeing so much of Tony?"

She shrugged. "Not really. It's silly since it was so far in the past, but it still hurts. I plan to, at some point, let him know how much of a jerk he was."

Kassie smiled more fully. "That will probably do you both good."

Kassie closed the dishwasher door and pressed the start button. She'd heard about Tony's cruel prank at the time. It wasn't because Kris had told her. They hadn't had the type of relationship where they'd shared secret crushes, or much of anything else, for that matter.

No, Kassie had known because everyone else had. Tony had shared the note Shannon had conned her into writing with all of his friends, who'd shared it with their friends. At least she'd only had to endure the taunts and jeers for a couple of weeks.

School had been almost over, and Tony's family had moved to Fort Walton Beach right after that.

Kassie hung the dishcloth over the handle of the oven door. "You're leaving your car parked in the garage till this is over, right?"

"Yeah." It would be a pain having to rely on Kassie and Tony for transportation, but since the killer knew what she drove, tooling around town in it would be reckless, if not downright stupid. Going anywhere alone wasn't too smart, either.

The ring of the doorbell cut across her thoughts, and she walked from the kitchen. "That's Tony."

"Check the peephole before you open the door." The admonition followed her into the living room.

It wasn't necessary. She was naturally cautious. Even more so now.

When she swung open the door, Tony stood on Kassie's porch in jeans and a burnt-orange polo shirt, his sandy blond hair mussed by the moderate breeze. The same attraction she'd felt in high school surged through her, and she tamped it down.

She gave him a relaxed smile. "I hope you're not going to regret this." If he expected to have the space over the charter office livable in time to sleep there tonight, it was going to be a long evening.

She didn't get a return smile. His mouth was set in a straight line and creases of worry marked his face. She dipped her gaze to a small stack of papers clutched in his right hand.

Kassie appeared beside her holding Gavin's hand. "Hi, Tony. Long time no see."

Instead of returning her greeting, he gave her a quick nod. "You ladies need to see something. May I come in?"

Kris's pulse kicked into high gear. Whatever he held, it wasn't good.

Kassie motioned toward the couch. "Have a seat."

Kris sat on one side of him, her sister

on the other. "Come here, sweetie." Kris patted her lap, and Gavin climbed into it.

When she looked down at what Tony held, her own face stared back at her. The image looked as if it had been blown up, making it somewhat grainy. What little background was visible was too blurred for her to identify where she'd been at the time the picture was taken.

"Where did you get that?"

"It was turned over to the police."

"By who?"

"A maid in a hotel in Holley."

She shook her head, more confused with every answer. "How did she get it?"

"She was cleaning a room, found a drawer full of photos. She recognized the missing camper from the news story and called the police. There were pictures of two other women, the homicide case I told you about and the woman we found in the woods."

"But why—" She swallowed the rest of the question. Her picture was there because she fit the profile. A wave of dread washed through her, chilling her all the way to her core.

She didn't have just the boater to fear. She'd somehow come to the attention of a serial killer. He knew where she was and had gotten close enough to take her picture.

Tony's grip tightened around what he held. "I'm ready to get you moved to the space over the charter office, and I fully intend to stay there with you. But I'd rather see you safely away from here."

"I don't know where to go other than Mark's parents' place." She squeezed Gavin against her chest. Anything that put her in danger threatened her little boy, too.

Tony looked at Gavin. "You might want to think about having him stay with someone else."

"As long as I've got your protection, I think he'll be safest with me." Dropping him off somewhere else was a poor option. He hadn't slept in his own room since Mark was killed. In fact, he wouldn't go to sleep without her lying down next to him.

Leaving him in someone else's care would add trauma on top of trauma.

She again lowered her eyes to what he held. "You have other pictures?" His stack looked like it contained at least three or four.

"There are three more." He slid the top one to the back.

In the next photo, she stood at a grill smiling over one shoulder, a long-handled spatula in her right hand.

"Wait. I recognize that picture. I was at Shannon's. This was a couple of months ago. We were grilling out after spending the day on her boat."

"You ladies were apparently being watched."

"No, Shannon took the picture. I was so windblown, I didn't want her to. I threatened to beat her with the spatula. Then to add insult to injury, she posted it on Facebook." She shook her head. "I never knew what she was going to do."

Pain stabbed through her. Shannon was one of a kind. That unpredictability made her fun. She was a cheerleader, a shoulder to cry on, a confidant—the best kind of friend.

Tony showed her the other two pictures, both ones she recognized as having been taken by Shannon.

She looked up at him. "I don't know about the first photo, but he got the others from Shannon's Facebook page. Her profile isn't public. The man who attacked her took her phone, so he had access to those pictures." It wouldn't have been difficult. Shannon had never set up a password to lock her phone.

Her heart was pounding in earnest now. "You know what this means? The boater is your serial killer."

"I think you're right. Everything you witnessed just might help solve this case."

She nodded. If her eyewitness account led to his capture, how many lives would be saved? Some serial killers' sprees went on for years. But would his capture be worth Shannon's death? Her parents wouldn't think so.

She shifted on the couch to face Tony more fully. "The killer didn't take those pictures. He hasn't found me." The cold dread that had seized her earlier released some of its grip.

Tony's jaw tightened. "He will. It's just a matter of time. He followed you as far as Navarre. I'm sure he's searching for you. How long do you think it'll be before he reaches Pensacola?"

Kris swallowed hard. Tony was right. The fact that the killer didn't know where she lived didn't mean she was safe.

Tony continued. "Now he has three reasons to kill you. He believes you saw him dump whatever he threw off of his boat. Chances are good it was a body. You're also a direct witness to Shannon's murder. If those aren't good enough reasons to come after you, he realizes you fit the profile of the girls he takes. He has targeted you to be one of his victims." He held up the stack of photos. "This is proof."

She pressed her lips together, the delicious meal Kassie had fed her congealing into a lump.

Kassie shifted at the other end of the couch. "You need to get somewhere safe, and the charter office isn't it."

"Anywhere I go, I'll be putting someone else in danger. Except for Mark's parents." The odds of the killer following her to Ohio were slim. The odds of him being able to get past her father-in-law and his arsenal of weapons were even slimmer.

She drew in a deep breath. "I'll message them on Facebook. They're already posting pictures galore, so they should see it soon. In the meantime, we need to move ahead with our original plan." She looked at Tony. "If you're still okay with sleeping on the couch in the office, I'll feel safe upstairs."

She'd stay holed up inside with Gavin and her dog. Kassie could pick up groceries or anything else she needed and also walk Bella. So could Tony.

Tony. She hadn't wanted to see him again. Now they were not only having daily contact, he was going to be sleeping right downstairs. Instead of consternation, the thought brought relief.

Regardless of everything that had happened in the past, his presence in her life now was a godsend. She would soon be at the charter office with Tony securing her safety. It was exactly where she needed to be, at least until Mark's parents returned and she could hightail it for Ohio.

Two weeks. With Tony's help, she could hang on that long. She would stay busy with the charter office duties and her son and her dog.

And she would try to not make herself crazy by focusing on the danger she was in.

Kris moved about the small kitchen in the back of the charter office. Gavin sat in his high chair a few feet away, playing with a couple of matchbox cars. Bella had already eaten and lay against the wall, almost out of her way, but not quite.

One small and one medium-size pan sat atop the two-burner stove, steam seeping out around their lids. The kitchen wasn't large enough or well-equipped enough for any gourmet cooking, but the pasta and spaghetti sauce that were almost ready would be more than sufficient.

Two nights ago, she and Tony had gotten Gavin's crib and a full-size bed from one of her spare bedrooms moved and assembled upstairs. They'd also packed up enough personal belongings to last the next two weeks.

Last night, they'd done some more cleaning upstairs and compacted everything even more so Gavin and Bella would have room to play. Between the kitchen and bathroom downstairs and the makeshift bedroom upstairs, she couldn't say it was comfortable, but it was livable. She'd made it through two days. Twelve to go. Eventually, she'd be counting off the hours.

Not only was she scared half out of her mind, staying cooped up inside was about to push her over the edge. From the time she was little, she'd always been an outdoor girl. Running with Gavin hooked into his stroller, going out on Shannon's or one of her dad's boats, working in her yard— it was where she recharged and found her peace.

The metallic click of the lock up front, followed by the alarm tone and four beeps told her Tony had arrived. Kassie had left fifteen minutes ago, knowing Tony was on his way.

Kris walked from the kitchen in time to see Tony step into the hall. He was carrying a TV, the handles of a plastic bag looped over one arm.

"You brought a TV?"

"And a DVD player, along with a collection of some of the older Disney movies."

Warmth swelled in her chest. He'd obviously made his movie choices with Gavin in mind.

Over the past two days, she'd come to the conclusion that he didn't dislike kids, he was just uncomfortable around them. Apparently, he didn't have friends or family members with little ones. Maybe he needed more exposure to find out they didn't break or bite.

Not that it would make a difference for her. In less than two weeks, she'd be on her way to Ohio and wouldn't return until the killer was behind bars. Between the composite the police had and her description of the truck, the case shouldn't drag on for long. Once they caught the killer and she returned, except for the occasional search and rescue operation, there would be no reason for her and Tony to continue to have contact.

The thought didn't bring the relief she would have expected it to. The more time they spent together, the more they were falling back into the camaraderie they used to share, and she was once again looking at him as a friend, one she still found attractive. But she was long past high school crushes.

Tony drew in a deep breath. "Dinner smells good."

"Spaghetti. The pasta has another two minutes."

Instead of continuing to the kitchen, he stepped into the office on the left, formerly her dad's, now shared by Kassie and her. "I had another reason for bringing the TV. Or if you don't have cable here, we'll use one of the computers. At the station today, they were talking about the storm headed this way."

"Storm?" She hadn't heard. Of course, she hadn't watched the news in the past two or three days, either.

He set the TV on one corner of the desk, opposite the computer monitor. "Yep, a tropical storm. It's probably been upgraded to a hurricane in the past couple of hours."

"Are we in the cone?"

"Not at the moment, but you know how these things can shift."

She nodded. Having lived in Florida all her life, she was no stranger to hurricanes. The devastation Michael caused when it hit their area in 2018 was still fresh in her mind.

Tony pulled a stack of movies and the

DVD player from the bag and placed them beside the TV. "What do you say we eat, watch a Disney princess fall in love, then see what we can find on the storm. If we can't find anything, we'll check the NOAA website."

"Sounds good."

She led him into the kitchen where Gavin was pushing his cars back and forth across the tray, making motor and crashing noises.

Tony gave him a couple of stiff pats on the shoulder. "Hi, Gavin." At least he was trying.

After draining the pasta, she dished up one large plate and one small one, then handed the tongs and serving spoon to Tony. A new sense of dread was now piled on top of the one that had been a constant companion for the past several days.

The storm was a good five or six days out. Maybe it would track even farther away and miss them entirely. Not that she wished it on someone else. She just had enough to worry about without dealing with hurricane prep, likely damage to her home and power outages that could go on for weeks.

After cutting up Gavin's spaghetti, she took the little metal cars and put his spoon and plate in front of him. When she'd sunk into her own chair, Tony sat opposite her, took Gavin's hand and reached across the table to take hers. She completed the circle by holding her son's hand.

She'd never shared a meal with any of the Sandersons without someone blessing the food. For the past two nights, that "someone" had been Tony. And it had felt good.

That comforting sense of family had struck her every time the three of them had joined hands, and she'd had to tamp down a longing she hadn't even known she'd had. Whatever she was longing for, it wasn't anything within her reach—not with Tony, maybe not with anyone. Her first responsibility would always be to her son.

Tony had just finished his prayer when

his ringtone sounded from inside his pants pocket. Before swiping and putting it to his ear, he glanced at the screen. "It's my dad."

While Tony talked, Gavin made some unsuccessful attempts to spoon spaghetti into his mouth before foregoing the utensil and using his fingers. Oh, well, she'd clean him up when they finished.

Tony ended the call and laid his phone on the table. "Dad has a large charter Monday afternoon, and his first mate has the flu. He's not likely to be over it by then. Since I've got tomorrow and Monday off, he asked if I could help him."

She nodded, pushing aside the vague sense of disappointment settling over her. He'd talked about hanging out with her at least part of both days. It would have helped pass the time.

He picked up his fork and took a bite. "Mmm. I'm guessing this didn't come out of a jar."

"It did, but I doctored it up."

"I can tell." He took a couple more bites. "You can cook for me anytime."

He gave her a smile of approval, and her stomach responded with a flutter. She promptly squashed it. "Thanks for the compliment."

He took a long swig of iced tea. "If we weren't trying to keep you hidden, I'd bring you with us on Monday's charter."

She looked at him with raised brows. "I'm afraid I'd turn you down on that one."

"Why? You love boating. It would be fun."

Was Tony really that clueless or was he goading her? "I love boating with Buck, our charter captain. I loved boating with Shannon. I have no interest in being on the same boat or even in the same town as your father."

Maybe that was harsh, but thinking about Jerry Sanderson's betrayal always brought out the worst in her.

Tony frowned. "My dad has nothing against you or your family. The animosity has always been one-sided."

She laid down her fork. "It was your father who broke up the partnership, not mine. Then he opened a competing business forty-five minutes away, doing everything he could to take all of my father's business with him. Then he spread all kinds of lies about my family."

Throughout her rant, Tony's eyes had grown wider, his jaw more slack. "What kind of lies?"

She opened her mouth to respond and snapped it shut again. The words to back up what she'd just said weren't there. Her father had made all kinds of accusations, but now that Tony had pinned her down, she couldn't remember him giving a single example.

She shrugged. "Just lies. I don't remember the details." *Wow, that was pathetic.* Time for a change in topic. "Any progress on Shannon's case?"

"Her cell phone provider got back to us. They pinged her phone and got nothing. The killer apparently took what he wanted and destroyed the phone."

She hadn't expected any different. Killers were usually smart enough to not walk around with their victims' phones.

When they'd finished eating, Tony insisted on washing their dishes since she had cooked. By the time he finished, she had Gavin cleaned up and dressed in his pajamas.

Tony met her in the hall. "Does Bella need to go out?"

"Not till bedtime. Kassie took her out before she left." She led him into the office and sat on the couch with her son. Bella lay at her feet.

Tony handed her the stack of movies. "Are there any of these Gavin hasn't seen?"

She looked through them—titles like *The Little Mermaid, Sleeping Beauty, Aladdin, Snow White* and *Beauty and the Beast.* When he'd finished plugging everything in and hooking the DVD player to the TV, she smiled up at him. "He's seen them all, but that's okay. He watches them over and over and never gets tired of them."

She handed him *Aladdin*, and he put it into the DVD player.

"I got all these from a guy I work with. I think his kids are older than we are. He originally had VHSs and sometime back traded them out for DVDs for his grandkids."

Over the next hour and a half, Gavin slid from her lap to nestle between Tony and her. By the time the movie ended, he was leaning heavily against her arm.

"I think he's asleep." She'd let him sleep until she was ready to go upstairs herself. She'd feel more secure if that upstairs room didn't have French doors leading onto a balcony. The doors were protected by the alarm, but still.

There was also the potential visibility from the street. The doors had curtains over them, but they were thin—only slightly more substantial than sheers. It was better than nothing, though. Anyone looking up from outside would only see vague shadows.

She twisted and shifted her son until

he lay across her lap. In this position, she could face Tony more fully.

"I really appreciate all you're doing, seeing to our safety."

"I don't mind a bit." He gave her an apologetic smile. "I'm hoping this makes up, at least a little, for my being so clueless in high school."

"It does. But it wasn't the clueless part that bothered me. It was the cruel part."

"What do you mean, *cruel*?"

"I'd had a crush on you our entire junior and senior years. Knowing you were leaving for Fort Walton Beach, Shannon insisted I should let you know and conned me into writing that note. Stupid, I know. But you could have just told me you weren't interested instead of trying to humiliate me with it."

He stood, shaking his head, confusion written all over his face. "What are you talking about?"

"Shannon said she gave you the note and you put it in your backpack."

His eyebrows drew together, forming

vertical creases between them. "Shannon didn't give it to me. I never saw it until someone showed it to me. I snatched it and kept it, hoping nothing would come of it. I didn't want anyone giving you grief over it."

She hesitated, doubt seeping into what she'd believed for so long. "Why would Shannon lie about it?"

"I don't know. But she didn't give it to me." He paced to the other side of the room and back again. It didn't take long. "All the time we spent studying together, did you ever know me to have a mean streak?"

"No." He'd been nice to everybody, had even stuck up for the underdog. But why would Shannon say she'd given him the note when she hadn't?

She inhaled sharply. Shannon hadn't come right out and said she'd given it to him. She'd said it was tucked securely into his backpack. Kris had assumed the rest. Did Shannon back out of giving it to him personally and instead slip it into his pack without his knowledge? If so, someone obviously noticed, took the note and shared it with the student body.

He looked down at her, his eyes pleading. "If I never had a mean streak, why would I intentionally destroy a friendship, one that I valued the way I valued ours?"

He spoke with such conviction, her chest squeezed. She'd thought he valued her friendship. She had certainly valued his. That was why the situation had hurt so badly. Was it possible she'd been angry with him all this time for something he hadn't done?

His confusion was so real, he had to be telling the truth. If she'd been wrong about him for so long, was it possible she'd been wrong about his father, too?

She swallowed hard. "I believe you."

His breath released in a rush. "Thank you."

The way they'd parted had obviously bothered him. It had bothered her, too. They could now renew their friendship without that ugliness hanging over them.

But that was all. Regardless of Shannon's prodding, considering anything more seemed like being unfaithful to Mark. Yeah, it was irrational, but that was how she felt.

Tony circled behind the desk and eased into the chair. "Since there isn't a cable hookup anywhere, how about if I bring up the NOAA website on the computer? I can angle this so you don't have to disturb your little one until you're ready to head upstairs."

After several clicks, he turned the monitor around. "Here we go."

She leaned forward to see what he'd pulled up. The eastern edge of the five-day cone barely touched Florida. Mississippi and Louisiana weren't likely to fare as well.

"I know this sounds really selfish, but I can't help but hope that cone moves even farther west or peters out altogether." Of course, the latter wouldn't happen. Over water, especially warm water, storms only gained strength.

He circled the desk again to sit on the couch, then squeezed her shoulder. "Whatever happens, we'll get through it."

We? That was what he'd said. And she didn't doubt it. He'd already proved he was willing to be there for her. She couldn't start depending on him, but for right now, she'd take whatever support he wanted to offer. For the past eighteen months, she'd faced every problem alone, and she was getting tired.

"What's on your agenda for tomorrow?" He'd already told her he wasn't working.

"Church in the morning. The services are live streamed, so we could watch it right here."

Another *we*. She'd pass on this one. "That's okay. You go ahead. I don't want to keep you away from your church." She'd rather do a Disney marathon than have to sit through Tony's church service. She got her fill of sermons with Kassie.

"I don't mind missing the service if I get to watch it here with you."

"That's all right. I'll read or do something with Gavin."

He lifted his eyebrows. "We used to go as kids and enjoyed it."

Yeah, they had. They'd even gone to the same church. His whole family had attended. Though Kris's dad had never gone, her mom had regularly taken her and her sisters. Then she'd stopped.

That had been her dad's fault. He'd always been jealous, convinced he'd lose her to someone else. Kris had thought he was imagining things, until her mother took off. Watching her walk away from her faith had shaken Kris's own. God taking her husband had dealt it the final death blow.

She scooped Gavin up in her arms and scooted forward on the couch. "I'm turning in. I need to get this guy in bed."

"I'll take Bella out for her final time tonight. Then I'll be ready to hit the sack, too." He cast the couch a sideways glance. "Such as it is."

She followed his gaze. It was a good

ten or twelve inches too short to accommodate his six-foot frame, but he hadn't complained once. Instead, he'd lain on his back, one knee bent, the other foot resting on the floor. By the time the two weeks were over, he was going to be glad to see her safely out of town, just to get back in a real bed.

She waited in the office while Tony slipped out the back door with Bella. The lock clicked over. The dog's potty breaks didn't take long. The parking lot occupied the space directly behind the building. Although the patch of grass bordering the sidewalk was a short distance away, it was still close enough for Tony to keep the back door in sight.

When he returned, she followed him down the hall with Gavin and waited while he peered out the plate glass window in the darkened lobby. They'd followed the same routine the past two nights, with Tony checking to make sure no one was within sight of the building. The kitchen window had vertical blinds, and the bathroom was windowless. But the large window in front was uncovered, as was the door. Since her stay was temporary and she was avoiding the lobby, they hadn't gone to the trouble of installing blinds.

"The coast is clear."

At Tony's words, she shifted Gavin to her hip to free one hand and slipped around the corner to the closed door. As soon as she swung it open, Bella shot around her and up the stairs.

When Kris gripped the handrail, ready to follow, Tony spoke behind her. "Are you okay carrying him?"

"I'll make it. I do this at home regularly."

"Your stairs at home would probably pass Florida building codes. These wouldn't."

He was right. They were far too steep. At the turn of the last century, laws were different from today.

By the time she reached the top, Bella was already stretched out in the middle of the bed. Kris bid Tony good-night with a wave and a tired smile, and he closed the door downstairs.

She approached the crib with her sleeping son. The forty-watt bulb in the simple ceiling fixture left a lot of the room in shadow, but that was okay. The dimmer the lighting, the lower her chances of being noticed from the street.

When she laid Gavin in his crib, he barely stirred. He'd likely sleep soundly all night. He'd started sleeping the night through at nine weeks old, and now at two, he rarely awoke before seven o'clock.

If only she could be so blessed. The past two nights, she'd woken almost every hour. She would blame it on being in a strange bed, but she hadn't slept any better at home. As soon as she hovered near sleep, the image of Shannon lying on the floor in a pool of blood would slam into her mind. If it wasn't that image, it was others—the decomposing body in the woods, skull smashed in; the pickup truck next to her, a killer at the wheel with murder in his eyes; the missing camper, vibrant and healthy one short week ago, likely now dead. When she slept, those same images invaded her dreams.

She moved back to the stairway to close and latch the safety gate. Having the door at the bottom of the stairs made sense when the upstairs space was used for storage. But a steep open stairway with an active little boy in residence was a recipe for disaster.

The safety gate had been Tony's doing. When they'd finished moving some things in and setting up the beds that first night, Tony had made a two-in-the-morning run to Walmart. Before three, he'd had the gate installed.

She flipped the light switch at the top of the stairs, and the room fell into virtual darkness. Once her eyes adjusted, enough light from the street filtered through the thin curtains to enable her to safely move around the room without the aid of the light fixture.

As heavily shadowed as everything was, the room didn't look half bad. She and Tony had gotten all the boxes stacked neatly against the back wall. Yesterday, Tony had shown up with a couple of huge plastic totes for all the miscellaneous pieces and stacked them next to the boxes. The only things too large to go into the totes were the vacuum, some fishing poles and a couple of wooden oars. He'd stood them up in the back corner.

At her insistence, they'd put Gavin's crib against the boxes. She wanted him as far away from the French doors as possible. It was probably irrational. If someone came through those doors, Gavin wouldn't be any safer at the far end of the room than in the middle, but positioning herself between the doors and her son couldn't be a bad thing.

Kris slipped into the T-shirt and yoga shorts she'd brought to sleep in. "Come on, Bella. Move over." She gave the dog a push. She didn't budge.

An adult golden retriever sprawled in the center of her king-size bed at home was okay. It wasn't going to work in a full-size bed, not if she expected to get any sleep.

"Okay, bed hog." She slid both hands under the dog and rolled her onto her back. "You're not taking your half out of the middle."

Once she had the dog situated, she picked up her Kindle from the box she'd repurposed as a nightstand. Maybe she'd eventually fall into a dreamless sleep.

The reading should help. The book she'd started earlier in the week was a romantic comedy. She was a quarter of the way through. What she'd read so far had offered a little bit of romance and a whole lot of comedy. Exactly what she needed.

She settled back with the book. Soon, soft snoring created a backdrop for her thoughts. It wasn't coming from the man downstairs. She had no idea whether Tony was asleep or whether he was a snorer.

Bella left her no doubt. *Great.*

She looked at her dog in the soft glow emitting from her reader. She lay stretched out on her side, facing the crib, her back to Kris. Gavin was still in the same position he'd been in when she'd laid him in the bed. That made two of them getting a good night's sleep.

She returned her attention to the story. She would read till her eyelids grew heavy. Just a little longer. If she didn't stop until she could no longer stay awake, maybe she'd actually sleep. Soon the words began to blur. Every time she blinked, her eyes stayed closed a little longer.

A soft rattle came from somewhere nearby. Her eyes shot open, and she lay frozen, body rigid, Kindle clutched face-down against her chest. What had she just heard?

She rolled her head toward the balcony. Beyond the filmy curtains, a shadow shifted. The next moment, both doors exploded inward with a crash, jerking a scream from her throat.

A man stood silhouetted against the light pouring in unobstructed from the street below, a knife clutched in one hand. The shrill squeal of the alarm filled the room.

Bella sailed off the bed amid a flurry of sharp barks. Kris rolled across the space just vacated by her dog and sprang to her feet next to Gavin's crib.

On the other side of her bed, dog and man stood facing off, about five feet apart. Bella stopped barking long enough to release some angry growls, then resumed.

The man advanced a step and swung the knife.

Kris's heart leaped into her throat. "Bella!"

The dog jumped back, her barking even more ferocious. She moved side to side in front of the intruder, blocking his way to her people. She would protect them or die trying.

The man advanced, swinging the knife, and Bella retreated. Kris leaned over Gavin's crib to snatch one of the wooden oars that stood in the corner and held it like she would a baseball bat. Bella backed around the foot of the bed and toward the crib. Kris released another long scream as her dog moved closer. Now Gavin's screams joined her own.

Less than a minute had passed since the intruder had broken through the doors, but already her time was running out. Backed against the wall between the bed and crib, there was no means of escape.

The knife slashed through the air again, and she swung the oar. He threw up his left arm to block the blow. The oar connected with a solid *thwack*.

The door at the bottom of the stairs creaked open. Relief surged through her. It was premature. The man made one more angry slash, this time at her rather than her dog. She jerked backward as the sharp tip of the blade grazed her throat. The sting barely penetrated her fear.

"Kris!" Tony's scream accompanied his pounding footsteps. But the intruder had already sailed over the bed and was running for the damaged doors.

Kris's knees buckled, and she dropped the oar. As Gavin's screams echoed through the room, she collapsed to the floor in a crumpled heap.

FIVE

Tony charged up the stairs, taking them two at a time, weapon drawn. He'd been dead to the world. Kris's scream had jarred him instantly awake. Her son's distressed cries and the squeal of the alarm had chased away any grogginess that might have remained.

Kris had screamed several times. She was now quiet, but sharp, frenzied barks came from beyond the latched security gate.

God, please let her be all right.

Instead of fiddling with the latch, he leaped over the barrier and into the room. Her son's screams quieted to soft sobs. Kris was sitting on the floor between her bed and his, one hand curled around the side of her neck. The balcony doors were wide open, and Bella was outside looking through the railing, her barks piercing the squeal of the alarm.

Ignoring the longing to comfort Kris, he ran onto the balcony. A large pocketknife was lying on the floor, the blade exposed. After stepping around it with little more than a glance, he peered over the edge of the railing, searching the street below. A figure disappeared around the corner of the building.

He pulled his phone from the pocket of his gym shorts. He'd put it there when he'd grabbed his weapon. The security company would have already notified the police, but he had something to add—a vehicle description.

When he stepped back into the room, Kris was on her feet, hand still pressed against her neck. She was wearing a T-shirt and a pair of those stretchy pants women often wore while exercising. Her hair was mashed down on one side and sticking up in spiky disarray on the other. The fear emanating from her twisted his heart.

He laid his weapon on top of one of the stacks of boxes and then dialed 911 as he approached her. "It was him, wasn't it?"

She nodded, eyes wide. Bella padded in from the balcony and circled the bed to press herself against Kris's leg. One of the wooden oars lay on the floor next to her. She'd apparently tried to use it as a weapon.

When the dispatcher came on, Tony explained what had happened and gave a description of the truck. They would put out an APB and have units search the area. Meanwhile, police would arrive any minute. If not for the alarm, they would probably already hear the squeal of approaching sirens.

"How about if we go downstairs, shut the alarm off and meet the police?"

She nodded, her eyes still wide. "He found me. He knows where I am. He tried to cut Bella." She lowered her hand and looked at it. "He cut me."

Panic stabbed through him, and he rushed toward her.

She held up her hand. "I'm okay. It's not much more than a nick."

His breath expelled in a rush. A blood smear marked her palm, a matching one on her throat. She was right. It wasn't bad, certainly not life-threatening. But that didn't dull the sense of protectiveness shooting through him, or tame the urge to wrap her in his arms and hold her until all threats were gone. Before he could act on the impulse, she turned to lift Gavin from the bed. Then she knelt to wrap one arm around her son and the other around her dog.

Yes, the killer had found her. The thought put a cold lump of dread in his chest. It probably hadn't even been that difficult. If he'd checked out Shannon's friends before destroying her phone, he'd have found Kris's profile and seen her name. *Richards* may not have led him anywhere, but an internet search of *Ashbaugh* would pull up the charter company. Finding her there would have been a long shot, but it was one that had paid off.

After retrieving his weapon, he led her toward the stairs, her son's hand tucked into hers. "We've got to get you somewhere safe."

"I know." Her voice was soft.

"Somewhere away from here."

She followed him down the stairs, matching her son's pace, one slow step at a time. At the bottom, she turned toward the hall, still holding Gavin's hand. "I'll be right back."

Tony continued across the room and punched the code she'd given him into the alarm panel by the front door. Now a more distant sound reached him, the scream of approaching sirens.

Kris reappeared a minute later and sank into the chair behind the desk. The blood smear on her throat was gone, an inch-long red line in its place, barely visible in the soft glow of the streetlights drifting through the window.

She dragged Gavin onto her lap. "I have

a friend from high school who moved to Texas. I haven't talked to her in ages, but we are Facebook friends. I could message her and see if she could put me up for the next week and a half."

"That sounds like a good plan." Anywhere except Florida. Georgia and Alabama, too, because they were both too close to Pensacola.

Tony moved to the front door to watch for the responding officers. Judging from the volume of the sirens, they were close.

Soon flashing blue lit up the street and reflected off the buildings. A Pensacola Police cruiser pulled into one of the parallel parking spaces in front, K-9 Unit displayed on the side. A German shepherd dog sat in the back. The driver door swung open, and a familiar figure climbed from the driver's seat.

Tony cast a glance at Kris. "The police are here, more specifically, your future brother-in-law."

"Jared?" Kris rose, letting Gavin slide from her lap, and approached the door.

As Jared moved closer, Tony hit the light switch. Relief flooded the other man's features. Kris swung open the door. After wrapping her in a hug, Jared held her away from him, looking her over. "You're all right?"

"Thanks to Bella and Tony."

"When the call was dispatched and they gave this address, I about had a heart attack."

As Tony watched the exchange, warmth filled him. Kris was obviously close to her future brother-in-law. From the little bit he'd seen, she was finally enjoying some closeness with her sisters, too, at least one of them. The constant friction he'd seen between the twins as teenagers seemed to have disappeared.

"Tell me what happened."

"The killer climbed onto the balcony, kicked in the doors. Bella charged at him, barking and growling, but he had a knife." She put a hand to her neck. "He got me, but just barely. I'm all right."

Tony's jaw tightened. "He apparently

dropped the knife on the balcony in his haste to escape."

Kris looked at him sharply. "He did? Maybe you can get prints."

"Maybe." It wasn't likely. If he'd worn gloves to kill Shannon, he'd have taken the same precautions coming after Kris.

Jared's thoughts had apparently followed the same track. "Could you see if he was wearing gloves?"

"Not really. The light was behind him. He was swinging the knife, and Bella was backing up, trying to stay out of his reach. There are a couple of paddles up there, like from a canoe or rowboat. I grabbed one and tried to club him with it, but he blocked it."

Tony smiled. "You were going to fight off a killer with an oar."

She returned his smile. "Only until you got up there with your gun. In the meantime, I was determined he wasn't going to get close enough to me or my son to use that knife."

Jared continued. "What happened then?"

"Tony headed up the stairs, and he took off." Her gaze met his. "I think he expected me to be alone. He wasn't counting on you or my dog."

As she talked, Jared made notes. "An APB has been issued, so units are searching for the truck. Can you tell me what he was wearing?"

"Blue jeans and a dark-colored shirt, black or navy blue, maybe even dark green."

"I take it you're positive it was the same guy you saw at your friend's house the night she was killed, and the one who came after you earlier this week?"

"I'm positive. Like on the road, he was wearing a bandana, his hair hidden underneath."

"Anything else you can tell us?"

"That's all I can think of."

"We'll take the knife into evidence, hopefully lift some prints, if not from tonight, maybe previously." He paused. "You're not going to stay here, are you?"

That last question came from Jared as a friend rather than an officer. Good, someone else to convince her to leave. Now it would be two against one. Except she'd already agreed to leave the state.

"I was thinking about getting in touch with a former friend who now lives in Texas."

Uh-oh. Tony frowned. "Was?"

"I'm having second thoughts."

"Why?" His exasperation came through in his tone. He should have known her agreeing to leave had come too easily. Kris had always been independent, someone who would balk at being put in a position to have to ask for favors.

She heaved a sigh. "If I leave, I'll escape for now, but eventually I'll have to come back. My life is here."

"If this guy gets a hold of you, you won't have a life to worry about." *Come on, Jared, help me out here.*

Kris continued. "He's killed four times in, what, the last three months?"

Tony pressed his lips together. Four

times that they knew of. It could be more. "Let's not make it five."

"My leaving isn't going to prevent that fifth killing. Likely, just the opposite. You don't have a single lead other than an old pickup truck with a bogus tag. And you wouldn't even have that if he hadn't come after me. With no leads and no idea when or where he'll strike next, how many women will have to die before you catch him?"

Jared put a hand on her shoulder. "You don't need to play the hero. If you can get somewhere safe, that's what you need to do."

Thanks, buddy. "Jared's right. You see to the safety of yourself and your son, and law enforcement will handle things here."

"I can't do that and live with my decision." Her gaze dipped to the floor. "I keep thinking about the woman we found in the woods and the woman you mentioned from Milligan who was killed the same way. I'm still haunted with thoughts of the camper we searched for on Monday, knowing she's probably lying in a shallow grave or in the woods somewhere."

Or at the bottom of the Gulf.

She looked up at him, her expression earnest. "Think about it. You're desperate to catch this guy. That's almost impossible without knowing when or where he's going to strike next. We still don't know the *when*, but we can anticipate the *where* because we know the *who*."

Tony shook his head. "Absolutely not. We're not going to use you as bait. You need to think about your son."

She bristled. "I *am* thinking about my son."

He winced. He hadn't intended to disparage her parenting skills, but he was desperate to make her listen to reason.

She heaved a sigh. "As long as this guy is out there, I won't be safe anywhere. It took him two days to find me. How long before he connects me with Mark's family? After tonight, I'm no longer sure he won't somehow track me down in Ohio. Here, I don't just have the police looking out for me, I have police who also happen to be personal friends of mine."

She put one hand on his shoulder, the other on Jared's. "I trust you guys to keep us safe."

Jared frowned. "We can't be with you twenty-four seven."

"Someone can. Maybe not with me, but watching." She dropped her hands. "I've thought about asking Kassie to let Gavin stay with her. But she would have to leave him with his babysitter while she works. I'm afraid it would be too easy for the killer to use him to get to me."

Tony pressed his lips into a thin line. She was right, on all counts.

"If I leave and more young women lose their lives at this guy's hand before he's caught, do you really think I could come back and pick up as if nothing happened? That's assuming I even make it back home. At this point, I can't guarantee that I would."

She'd made her point well. He didn't

even have a valid argument. But that didn't mean he had to like it.

He gave her a sharp nod. "We'll talk to the folks in charge and come up with a game plan."

Whatever they decided, he'd make sure she had ample protection.

He'd thought God had brought her back into his life so he could make right what he'd messed up in the past. But that wasn't the only reason. He'd also been put here at this specific time to protect her, maybe even to help guide her back to the faith she'd once had but rejected.

Was there another reason that he hadn't considered? The attraction was definitely there. So was the deep friendship they'd always shared, which made a good foundation for any romantic relationship.

No, no matter how much his heart was urging him otherwise, he wouldn't even consider it. She had a kid. After his niece had died while in his care, no way would he put himself in a position where he would be responsible for little Gavin.

Anything beyond their simple friendship was off the table.

He'd keep reminding himself of that fact. Daily.

Hourly, if he had to.

Jerry Sanderson turned the boat into the waves and hit the throttle. The bow rose, cutting a path through the choppy surface.

Kris closed her eyes and tilted her head back, relishing the sun on her face and the wind in her hair. In another hour, they'd be back at the marina in Fort Walton Beach where Sanderson kept his three boats.

Though she'd had no desire to spend the day on the water with Tony's father, here she was. She'd come along because she'd felt that she had to.

It wasn't that she owed Tony's father anything, because she didn't. But she owed Tony, big time. Even though two unmarked units would be watching the Ashbaugh Charters office, after Saturday night's incident, he'd been ready to renege on his offer to help with the charter, refusing to leave her alone. With everything he was doing for her, no way was she going to force him to choose between her and his father.

As much as she hadn't wanted to come, it hadn't been bad. Jerry Sanderson had been too occupied with his customers and captaining the boat to interact with her much beyond welcoming her aboard and flashing her the occasional friendly smile. Tony was staying pretty busy with his first-mate responsibilities, too.

That was all right. Just being on the water was entertainment enough. After being holed up in the charter office for the past four days, she'd have almost agreed to get on a boat with Jack the Ripper for an opportunity to soak up some sunshine. Even Gavin had seemed to be getting cabin fever. Her usually easygoing, compliant child had been especially disagreeable since yesterday.

She opened her eyes to look at her son, who was sitting in the lap of one of the customers, eyelids at half-mast, fingering the beads on her bracelet. Nineteen-year-old Emily had no interest in fishing and had signed up for the charter only because her boyfriend had. As someone who loved kids, it hadn't taken her long to decide that she'd rather play with Gavin than hold a fishing pole.

The rest of the group consisted of two women and four men. All seven were Florida State University students enjoying the last week of their summer break before the start of the new school year.

Tony moved from his position next to the helm to sit beside her. "Have you enjoyed yourself?"

"Totally. I'm glad I came." Not that she'd felt she had a choice. But Tony would be glad to know the afternoon hadn't been drudgery.

Being a nonpaying passenger, she hadn't felt right using the Sanderson bait and equipment, but at Tony's insistence, she'd done a little fishing herself. She'd had some nibbles that had resulted in nothing but lost bait. So she'd finally put up the pole and kicked back to relax. It was what she'd been doing ever since.

She looked out over the water, with its moderate chop, then up where puffy, white clouds were scattered across a blue sky. The sun was about two-thirds of the way through its descent, leaving them plenty of daylight left to make it in. She and Tony would even be back in Pensacola before dark.

Some distance off their starboard bow, another boat paralleled their path. Jared had agreed to remain a short distance away in his own boat, keeping watch and making sure no one got too close. He was no doubt armed and ready to use whatever he was carrying.

Tony smiled at Gavin, whose eyes were now closed. "I think we wore out your little one."

"We did." A hint of pink stained her little boy's cheeks and upturned nose. Florida sun could be brutal, especially in August. But Gavin wasn't sunburned; she had him too well slathered. The same windburn likely marked her own cheeks.

When they got back to the marina, Emily stood and passed her sleeping bundle off to Kris. Gavin stirred then rested his head on her shoulder and was out again.

Each of the charter customers said their thanks and goodbyes and filed off the boat.

Jerry Sanderson put a hand on Kris's shoulder. Kindness filled his eyes, and the smile he wore crinkled the skin at their corners. "I enjoyed having you and your little boy spend the afternoon with us. Thanks for coming."

"Thanks for having us." She turned to step off the boat. She didn't want to like this man, but it was hard not to. The warmth and acceptance she sensed from him cast doubt on all the negative things her father had said about him.

His voice halted her escape. "I was really sorry to read about your father's arrest and drug charges."

She turned to look at him. The sincerity in his words was reflected on his face. Suddenly the image she'd created of the Sandersons sitting around the dinner table disparaging the Ashbaughs and gloating over Bobby Ashbaugh's downfall no longer seemed plausible.

She shifted Gavin onto her hip. "Did you know before what he was involved in?"

"I had my suspicions. That's why I split with him and went off on my own."

She frowned. "And took a lot of Ashbaugh business with you."

"I didn't take a single name, phone number or email address. When I walked away, I completely started over. I did a lot of advertising to get the word out, and God blessed my efforts."

She narrowed her eyes. "You're telling me you didn't trash my father's reputation in the community?"

"I told my wife. I felt she deserved to know why I was breaking off an eight-year partnership."

Kris looked at Tony. "Did you know that's why they split?"

"Not until just now."

She looked from Tony's father to Tony and back to his father. Sanderson didn't even tell his sons? Everything he was saying was in complete opposition to what her father had told her for years.

More lies piled on top of all the others. Over the past few months, her father had shattered every ounce of trust she'd ever had in him.

She met Mr. Sanderson's gaze. "I'm finding out I've spent a lot of years believing lies."

He gave her a sad smile. "I'm sorry. We've been praying for you and your sisters. And since finding out what you've been through this week, we're really doubling down on those prayers."

She turned an accusing glare on Tony and then softened it immediately. He wasn't sharing personal information about her for no reason. He'd have had to tell his dad something about why he was dragging her along on today's charter. Coming from

Tony, whatever excuse he gave would be nothing but the truth.

"Thank you." She meant it. Not that she believed in prayer, but it was the thought that counted.

After saying their farewells, they walked to where Tony had parked his Tundra. Kris buckled Gavin into his car seat and climbed into the front. Tony slid into the driver's seat and cranked the engine. "How about we stop somewhere and pick up dinner when we get back to Pensacola so you don't have to cook."

"I'm all for that." She loved to cook, but not after a day on the water, especially with the added stress of having to spend it with Tony's father. Of course, that was stress that had turned out to be unnecessary.

Less than an hour later, Tony drove slowly down Government Street, approaching the charter office. "Did you notice the dark SUV we just passed?"

She looked in the side mirror. "Parallel parked on this side of the street?"

"Yep. That's one of ours."

She nodded. It sat facing Ashbaugh Charters, on the opposite side of the road, a short block away. With the fading sunlight and the tint of the windows, she couldn't see the occupants. "They're keeping an eye on the building?"

"Yep. I'm sure there's an unmarked unit in back, too, like this one—not close enough to be obvious but where they can still see the back door."

He'd told her yesterday that they were there. Seeing one of them for herself brought a lot of relief.

Thanks to Tony and his brother, Nick, the building had been secure by midafternoon yesterday. On his way to church, Nick had stopped by Lowe's and then dropped off wood and other materials to replace the damaged door jamb. After lunch, Tony had gotten everything fixed and working properly again. Fortunately, the doors themselves had been salvageable.

Between the materials delivery and actually performing the work, Tony had brought up his church service on the TV in the office. When he'd asked her to join him, she'd made up some excuse about needing to bathe Gavin. Then she'd felt guilty and ended up coming in to sit with him near the end of the service.

Mark had tried to get her to attend, too. He'd become a Christian shortly before the accident. Maybe he'd have had an impact on her eventually. Unfortunately, God took him before that could even start to happen.

As they drew closer to the building that housed the charter office, Kris's chest tightened. A burgundy Sorento sat parked in one of the parallel spaces in front of the building. "Kassie's still here."

"At almost seven thirty?"

Her stomach drew into a knot. Kassie had been at the charter office when she'd left late that morning with Tony. Why would she still be there, especially with everything that had been going on?

Granted, it wasn't dark yet. It was just

nearing dusk. And police were watching the place. But why tempt fate?

Tony eased into a spot across the street. The charter office lights weren't on. The lights next door were.

Kris released a relieved breath. Kassie was apparently showing the retail space and apartment above to a potential renter.

"I'm going to check on her. Can you come along?"

"If you hadn't asked, I would have insisted."

They crossed the street, and when Kris stepped inside, the door at the bottom of the stairs was open a full ninety degrees. Two voices came from above, Kassie's and a male voice.

The layout of this space was the same as in the charter office—narrow stairway leading to the upper story. On this side, though, the apartment above had been refurbished years ago to include a kitchenette and a small bathroom.

Tony pulled the door shut behind him,

and Kassie's voice grew closer. "So, what do you think?"

"It's perfect. I'll have the music store I've been wanting to open for ages and be able to live above it."

Good. It looked like they were going to finally have the place rented. The monthly payments would help cover some of the expenses, and in her situation, having a close neighbor held a lot of appeal.

"That sounds great." Kassie started down the stairs. With the angle of the door and where she was standing, Kris couldn't see her, but her sister's footfalls on the stairs told her where she was.

Then heavier footsteps joined the lighter ones, and their future renter continued. "The lease on my apartment in LaGrange isn't up for another four weeks. If I pay you this month's rent, will you hold it for me?"

"How about we say half and call it even? I'm glad to have you back."

Back? So it was someone they knew. Even better.

Kassie stepped around the door, and the smile she was wearing broadened. "Oh, hey, I didn't know you guys were back."

"We just got back. I saw your car parked out front and the lights on in here and figured—"

She swallowed the rest of her words when their new renter followed Kassie into the lobby.

Kassie squared her shoulders. "Kris, I'm sure you remember Spencer Cavanaugh."

Her voice was a couple of pitches higher than normal, and her pose said she was preparing for a battle.

"Yes, I remember." Where Kassie's tone was higher and tension-filled, her own was low and cold. "Hello, Spence."

Of course she remembered him. Druggie, wannabe rock star and their younger sister Alyssa's no-good former boyfriend. And Kassie was agreeing to rent to him? Had she lost her mind? His music store would probably be a front for a drug operation or prostitution ring or something equally seedy. If that was who her close neighbor was going to be, she could live without one.

Kassie introduced the two men, who hadn't previously met. Besides Spencer being two years behind them in school, their circles of friends hadn't intersected. Tony had run with the good kids. Spence... hadn't.

Kris looked at Tony and Spence. "Can you excuse us for a few minutes?"

She grabbed Kassie's wrist and led her out the front door. The SUV was still there, parked a short distance away. They'd be safe standing out front long enough for her to talk some sense into her sister, who had somehow lost hers.

"You're not seriously thinking of renting to him, are you?"

"He's not the same man we knew seven or eight years ago."

"And you can somehow guarantee that he's not going to be dealing drugs out of our building?"

"He won't."

"How do you know?"

"He's changed. He's not even a drug *user* at this point. He's spent six years serving our country."

Kris frowned. So he'd been in the military. That didn't mean that once he got away from the discipline and back in his hometown he wouldn't return to his former lifestyle. After all, how many times had she and Kassie gotten their hopes up that Alyssa was finally going to get her act together, only to be disappointed?

"He's even playing guitar with his church's worship team now."

Great. No wonder Kassie was all gung ho about renting to him. She probably figured he was one more person she could get to try to influence her wayward sister.

Maybe Kassie was right, though. If he really had changed, it wasn't right to hold the things he did as a teenager against him. But now that she was thinking about it, what irritated her the most was the fact that Kassie had made the decision without her input.

She crossed her arms. "You should have

talked to me. Decisions related to the charter business, we make together."

"I'm sorry. It's just that Spence and I have been talking for the past hour. That's why I'm here so late. I knew that once you got reacquainted with him, you'd agree with me."

She still wasn't ready to let it go. "Just remember, when he destroys the place or we've got cops making drug busts right next door to us, it's all going to be on you."

She spun and stalked to the door. When Kassie followed her inside, Spence lifted his brows. "Should I be warming up my pen, or is our verbal agreement off?"

Kassie tilted her head to the side. "Before you sign the lease, my sister might need some convincing."

Spence nodded. "I can understand that." He locked gazes with Kris. "I provided your sister with some references—my employer, my current landlord. I've only had one since my discharge from the army. I'm happy to answer any questions you might have for me, too."

Kris asked about his military background, his work, his friends, his activities, even his involvement with his church. Within thirty minutes, she was as convinced as Kassie apparently was. He really had changed.

Maybe dumping Alyssa was the smartest thing the man had ever done.

SIX

Tony got a Coke from the vending machine, popped the top and took a long swig. Several counties were working together trying to solve the string of murders and had almost nothing.

The crime scene investigators had been able to lift prints from the handle of the knife, but there'd been no match in IAFIS. Either their killer had never been arrested or he'd worn gloves and someone else had handled the knife before he had. Kris had been right. Their greatest chance of catching him was watching for him to come after her again.

He walked toward his captain's office. He'd check in before calling it an afternoon.

When he rapped lightly on the open

door, Keith looked up from the papers on his desk. "Come in. We just got word from Fort Walton Beach."

Tony eased into one of the chairs opposite the desk, his heart beating faster. "Yeah?"

"Some fisherman snagged a body. Young woman, slender, dark hair, head smashed in with a blunt object. She had a concrete block tied around her waist. They're waiting for positive identification, but she fits the description of your missing camper."

Tony nodded. "It would make sense. The dogs lost her trail at the Blackwater River and were never able to pick it up again. The Blackwater River flows all the way to the Gulf. Did they say where they found her?"

"Not too far from the inlet between Destin and Okaloosa Island, where Choctawhatchee Bay connects to the Gulf. The location was about a half mile from the location your lady friend pointed out. Either she'd missed it by a little bit or the body had drifted."

Even though he hadn't expected any different, the news was still like a kick in the gut. He knew her name—Julia Morris. He'd studied her picture and searched for her with the others, hoping the day would somehow have a positive outcome.

He pressed his lips together. "That makes three, same profile, all killed the same way."

"Four, counting the woman he stabbed to death last week."

And he was determined to make Kris number five.

"We're watching her." Keith had just read his mind. He knew about their long-time friendship, but if he suspected that there was anything more than that, he was wrong.

Keith leaned back in his chair. "We're watching her too closely for him to get anywhere near her, but hopefully not closely enough to tip him off." He paused. "I'll keep you in the loop, in addition to the regular briefings."

"I appreciate it."

As he walked through the parking lot toward his vehicle, he put a call through to Kris. She answered after the first ring.

"I'm heading your direction now. Anything you want me to pick up?"

"Milk. Other than that, we're good. I've been holed up in the office answering calls this afternoon. It's about time to close up, so Kassie's going home, and I'm getting ready to start dinner."

"What are we having?"

"Chicken Alfredo."

"I'll be there in twenty minutes."

She was feeding him another one of his favorites. This protection detail he was on had some great benefits. He'd had more home-cooked meals in the past week than he'd had in the past twelve months. He was going to be disappointed to see it come to an end and not just because she was feeding him well. He was really enjoying her company. Once they caught the man and the danger to her was over, he'd do everything he could to maintain the friendship they'd reignited. He'd somehow just have to keep a rein on his emotions.

That hadn't been a problem before. She'd always been nothing but a friend—one of the best. He'd dated other girls, but pursuing a romantic relationship with Kris had never crossed his mind.

That had changed. She was a woman now, and an attractive one at that. After ten years apart and all the time they were spending together, it was getting harder and harder to continue thinking of her as simply a friend.

He disconnected the call and slid into the driver's seat. He hadn't wanted to leave her at all. But he couldn't very well park himself at the charter office twenty-four seven. He had to leave her safety in the hands of the officers keeping watch. And the Lord. He was doing plenty of that, too—he'd been sending up pleas for her protection for the past week.

When he arrived at the charter office, Kassie was just leaving. He greeted her at the door.

"Good day, I assume?"

"Yep, uneventful."

"Those are the kind to have."

As soon as he stepped inside, mouthwatering aromas wafted to him. His stomach growled. That sandwich and chips he'd eaten at lunchtime were long gone.

He locked the door behind him and set the alarm. When he reached the kitchen, Kris stood at the stove stirring something in a pot, her back to him. The contents of another pot were boiling, judging from the steam pouring out. Probably pasta, or maybe the chicken if she hadn't cooked it in advance.

He squeezed past her to put the milk he'd bought in the small fridge. "Dinner smells wonderful."

She cast him a sideways glance without halting her stirring of whatever was in that pot. "Thanks. It'll be ready in about forty-five minutes. It would be sooner if I wasn't limited to two burners."

He scanned the small kitchen. Bella lay under the table against the wall. A carton of heavy whipping cream and an open one-pound box of butter sat on the counter next to a grater that had small bits of what looked like parmesan cheese clinging to it. There wasn't a store-bought jar in sight.

"You're making it from scratch. I thought you were going to do things the easy way while here."

"You can't get much easier than Alfredo."

"Can I help you with anything?"

"I appreciate the offer, but more than one person moving about this kitchen is a crowd. You can just have a seat and keep me company. I'd say you could entertain Gavin, but he's pretty good at entertaining himself."

"How about Bella? Can I feed her?"

"I already did before I started cooking, and Kassie took her out before she left."

He squeezed past her again to take a seat next to her son. The little boy sat in his high chair, a coloring book open on the tray in front of him and a fat red crayon clutched in one hand. Seven other crayons were scattered about the tray, the empty box lying in the corner.

"What are you coloring there, buddy?"

"A house and a twee." He put the red crayon to the paper and began coloring in the leaves of the tree. Maybe it was fall in his picture. In North Carolina.

He picked up a yellow crayon and pointed to the object in the forefront of the picture. "Doggie."

"Is that Bella?" He had the color right.

"No, 'nother doggie."

Instead of coloring the dog, he moved the yellow crayon back and forth across the roof of the house.

Kris cast him another glance. "How was work?"

"Not bad. I handled a couple of new cases—a house robbery and a sexual assault."

"I thought homicide detectives just handled murders."

"That's how it is in large cities, but in smaller towns, detectives handle all kinds of investigations."

Kris moved to the fridge and pulled a plastic package from the freezer. "Do you like spinach?"

"Not by itself, but in Alfredo I do."

"Good. Otherwise, I could substitute broccoli."

"Either one is fine." In fact, he'd eat whatever she wanted to cook.

"They found the missing camper."

She spun to face him, hope in her eyes.

"Some fisherman snagged her body this morning."

Her shoulders drooped, and she seemed to deflate. "I hate that. I really didn't expect anything different, but I was still holding out a sliver of hope that she'd somehow turn back up alive and well. At least now her family will have some closure. Not that that's any real consolation." She paused. "Where did they find her?"

"About a half mile from the place you pointed out to them."

She nodded. "I was close."

"You did good."

When she had dinner ready, she took the

coloring book and crayons away from her son. He didn't protest. Of course, the same delicious aromas that had been tormenting Tony had probably been teasing Gavin for the past forty-five minutes.

Kris put a small spoonful of pasta on a plate and, after spooning the chunky sauce over the top, placed the plate in front of her son. When Tony carried his own food to the table, Gavin hadn't touched what was in front of him. Instead, he was sitting with his hands folded, obviously waiting for someone to say grace. That someone would be him, as it had been for the past week.

Gavin really was a good kid. Kris was doing an amazing job of raising him by herself. Someday God would bring a man into her life, someone who would be worthy of the love of both her and her sweet little boy. He prayed that would be a godly man who would restore her faith in God and people.

After Tony had blessed the food, Kris

picked up her fork. "Have you heard any more about the storm?"

"I haven't seen it for myself, but they say the track has been moved farther east."

She leaned back in her chair, face creased with concern. "That puts us in the cone."

"It's also been upgraded from a Cat. 2 to a Cat. 3." Not to compound her worries, but she needed to be prepared.

The creases deepened. "I'm worried about my house. It's right on the water and has those French doors across most of the back, not to mention all the windows."

"Do you have storm shutters?"

"I do. They're in the garage, but it's a huge job getting them installed. Mark and I helped Dad do it for Michael."

"I think we're still looking at landfall late Thursday night." He pulled his phone from his pocket.

"Who are you calling?"

"Dad and then Nick."

A few minutes later, he disconnected the second call and laid the phone facedown on the table. "It's settled. Dad and Nick will meet us there at two o'clock tomorrow afternoon. They're bringing Mom and Joanne, too."

"Joanne?"

"Nick's wife."

For several moments, Kris didn't say anything. Her eyes grew moist, and she blinked several times. Finally, she spoke. "Doesn't everybody have their own preparations to make?"

"I don't have anything to do except stocking us up on supplies. That's one advantage of apartment living."

"But your dad and mom don't live in an apartment, and I'm guessing Nick and Joanne don't, either."

"They don't, but they assured me they'll be able to get it all done."

"Tell them thank you, and I'll feed everybody."

"That sounds like a fair trade."

When they'd finished eating and cleaned up the mess, Bella and Gavin followed them to the office, which was also doing duty as a combination living room and guest bedroom. Tony sat at the desk to navigate to the NOAA website.

"After we see what this storm is doing, what do you say we watch another Disney movie? Gavin can pick this time."

"That sounds good."

As soon as she sat on the couch, Gavin climbed onto her lap and Bella lay at her feet. An image filled the monitor, much scarier than the last time he'd checked.

"The track is quite a bit farther east." He turned the monitor around. "We're right in the middle of the cone. Unless it totally hooks to the right in the next thirty-six hours, I'm afraid we're going to get slammed." There was probably plenty of news footage of the areas that had already been hit, but seeing it wouldn't do Kris any good. He walked around the desk. "Let's watch that movie now." After handing the stack to Kris, he smiled down at her little boy. "What movie do you want to watch?"

Kris thumbed through them, and Gavin snatched one from the stack. "Boody and Beast."

Tony took the case from him. *"Beauty and the Beast* it is."

After turning the monitor back around and moving the TV to the center of the desk, he slipped the DVD into the player. When he'd taken his place on the couch, Gavin slid from Kris's lap.

"Where are you going, sweetie? Let's sit in Mommy's lap and watch the movie."

Tony watched the little boy as he looked from him to his mother and back to him again. Maybe he didn't want to watch the movie. In that case, Kris would have to find something else to entertain him.

After one more glance at his mother, the little boy pointed at him. "Tony."

The next moment, he was climbing into Tony's lap.

Tony stiffened, one hand gripping the arm of the couch, the other curled into a fist. His heart pounded as if he'd just taken a flight of stairs at a full run.

More than fourteen months had passed since he'd last held a little one. He'd always loved kids and had jumped at the chance to babysit his niece. Then the un-thinkable had happened.

Nick and Joanne didn't blame him. They'd insisted it wasn't his fault, that SIDS was a silent killer that struck with no warning. It didn't matter what they said because he'd never been able to stop blaming himself.

"Tony?"

He released the breath he'd been hold-ing and looked at Kris. Her eyebrows were raised, and silent question filled her dark eyes.

"He won't bite. He won't break, either."

Wouldn't he? How could she be so sure? Little Zoe did.

"He's potty-trained, too. You don't even have to worry about being wet on." She gave him a smile, but he couldn't bring himself to return it.

Her smile faded, and she stood to lift her son from his lap.

"Tony." The little boy's voice held a note of protest. He tightened his fingers around Tony's shirt, instantly losing his grip when Kris straightened with him.

"What's the deal with you and kids?"

He shrugged, the motion feeling awkward. "I'm just not comfortable around them."

"It's more than that. You act like you're scared of them."

He winced. She was too perceptive. But he wasn't about to tell her his deepest, darkest secret. He hadn't told anyone outside his family.

"Something happened, didn't it?" The words were soft, barely above a whisper.

He didn't respond.

"Tony?"

"Let it go." He spoke through clenched teeth.

"If you want to talk about it, I'm a good listener."

He shot to his feet. "No, I don't want to talk about it." His voice was raised, the words sharp, but he couldn't seem to soften them. He had no desire to open old wounds, and she shouldn't be pushing him. It wasn't any of her business anyway.

He brushed past her and into the hallway. As he stalked into the lobby, a knock on the front door sent his heart into his throat and instantly dissolved his irritation.

He skidded to a stop. If whoever was there posed a threat, the officers standing guard outside would have been on him before he could reach the front door.

He peered through the panes of glass in the French-style door as he approached. Relief whooshed through him. Now he recognized the visitor. He was the owner of one of the neighboring businesses. Tony had seen him coming and going a couple of times. Tonight he was holding a large box.

Tony shut off the alarm and opened the door. "Yes?"

"I have something for Kris. It was delivered to me by mistake, left at my front door. I've had it since midafternoon, but I got busy and couldn't make it over here. When I was leaving, it looked like there was a light on in the back over here, so I figured I'd give it a shot."

Tony looked down at what the man held. It didn't have a UPS or FedEx label. Instead *Kristina Ashbaugh-Richards* had been written across the top with a black Sharpie, the charter office address below. There was no return name or address. His chest tightened around a growing lump of dread.

The man held up the box. "Do you mind giving it to her?"

"Sure. Thanks." If there was a bomb inside, the man would likely be in pieces, scattered all over Government Street, instead of standing on the charter office doorstep.

Tony swallowed hard and took the box. It weighed so little it almost felt empty. Whatever was inside was soft, judging from the muffled sounds it made when he tipped the box. Maybe he should see what was inside before giving the box to Kris. Would she perceive that as an invasion of her privacy? If so, he'd apologize later.

He'd just add that apology to the other

one he owed her. Now that he'd calmed down, he had to admit that he shouldn't have snapped at her. She was only offering a listening ear, something that, if he knew Kris, would have come with ample amounts of moral support.

First, he needed to see what was in the box.

When he turned around, Kris was standing at the end of the hall, Gavin in her arms. "What did Don bring over?"

"I don't know yet. There's no shipping label and no return address, which I find a bit suspicious. Would you like me to open it?"

"Please."

He set the box on the lobby desk and pulled the scissors out of the desk caddy. While he sliced through the tape sealing it, Kris remained standing at the end of the hall rather than venturing into the lobby.

He lifted the flaps and sucked in a sharp breath.

"What is it?" Kris's voice held a slight quiver.

"A stuffed animal."

She lowered Gavin to the floor and moved closer. When her eyes met Tony's, she hesitated.

The item in the box wasn't a gift. It was a threat, one with a whole lot of rage behind it.

Kris had thwarted his attack not once, but three times. First, she ran from him at Shannon's, leading to him being struck. She evaded him traveling on US 98. Then he couldn't get to her at the charter office because she had Tony's and Bella's protection. She was a witness. She fit the profile, and he wanted her badly. Now, he was furious.

Yes, the box held a stuffed animal, a dog. At least that was what it had been, before someone had gone crazy with a knife. Soft white stuffing was mixed with chunks and strips of blond fur. If the legs and tail were somewhere in the mess, he couldn't see them.

The head, though, had been left intact,

leaving no doubt as to the breed. It was a golden retriever.

"Tony?" Kris's tone held hesitation mixed with a solid dose of dread.

Gavin grasped the hem of her shirt and molded himself against her leg, obviously picking up on his mother's fear. As she moved closer, Tony fought the urge to close the flaps on the box, to tell her it was nothing. Anything to keep from upsetting her.

She would never let him get away with it.

When she reached his side, she grasped his arm, likely for support, then dipped her gaze to the contents of the box. A tortured wail poured from her and ended in a sob. Gavin burst into tears next to her.

After taking two steps back, she picked up her son and squeezed him to her chest, silent tears streaming down her face. Tony wrapped his arms around both of them, and Gavin's wails quieted to sobs.

He pressed his face to the top of Kris's head and whispered into her hair. "It's okay. I'm right here. I won't let him hurt either of you or your dog."

But was it a promise he would be able to keep? As diligent as he'd been, the killer had still come into her room while he'd been asleep downstairs. He would have to figure out a better way to protect her. Later.

Right now, Kris needed his comfort as much as his protection. So did her sweet little boy.

For the next several minutes, he held them, comforting and consoling them, offering reassurances.

And trying hard to not think about the longing that rose up inside him or how good it felt to hold them both in his arms.

Tony stood at the grill, his father and brother on either side of him. A couple of Pensacola PD officers were nearby keeping watch, hidden by shrubbery and other natural barriers. Someone was out front, too, watching from their vehicle. He hadn't seen the two in back in quite some time, but when he'd made a quick run to Publix for some salad fixings an hour ago, the vehicle in front had still been sitting at the edge of the road one door down.

It had been a good day. The six of them had worked in pairs getting all the shutters installed on the lower floor. Then Tony and Nick had worked from ladders to take care of the upper story while their dad had stayed on the ground to hand the panels up to them. None of them had wanted the women clinging to ladder rungs fourteen feet off the ground.

Now shutters protected every window and door except the front entry door, and Kris's generator was loaded into the back of his Tundra. Since she wouldn't be staying at her house, she was letting Kassie use it. If they lost power and it wasn't restored soon, he'd clean out her refrigerator and bring her food to Kassie's.

Currently, she was inside the house, hard at work on the rest of that dinner she'd promised, with the assistance of his mom and Joanne.

Gavin and Bella were inside, too, along with Gavin's babysitter. Kris had contacted her before they'd left the charter office, and the older woman had entertained both Bella and Gavin while the rest of them had worked.

Tony still hadn't told Kris that he was sorry for snapping at her last night. An apology would require an explanation. It was a conversation he'd been starting to prepare himself for while standing in the charter office lobby.

Then he'd looked in the box.

They'd eventually watched the movie, at Kris's suggestion. It had provided a good distraction for Gavin. He wasn't sure about Kris, but it hadn't done a thing for him. Not that he wouldn't have found it entertaining under different circumstances.

Nick elbowed him in the side. "You think you ought to flip that last steak before it's completely charcoaled on the one side?"

He slid the spatula under the ribeye and made a quick flip of his wrist.

"Sorry, a little distracted." Maybe he should let Nick man the grill.

Nick gave his shoulders a brotherly squeeze. "You've got reason to be, especially after last night's threat. Joanne and I are praying for you guys."

"Thanks."

"We're not praying only for protection."

"What do you mean?"

"Have you considered the possibility that God might have brought you back into her life for more than protection?"

"I don't know if she's even a Christian. Best-case scenario, she has strayed far from whatever faith she may have had as a child." Had his brother forgotten the command to not be "unequally yoked"?

"Maybe you're supposed to be salt and light for her."

He could go along with that. She'd given him a flat-out no when he'd asked her to watch his church service with him, but then she'd conceded. Granted, she'd missed most of the service, but it was a start. He wouldn't give up working on her, either.

"Your brother is right."

Great. Now his dad was chiming in, making it two against one.

His dad continued. "Kris has been through a lot. Besides losing her husband, she's been failed by some of the Christians in her life. Her mother walking out on her had to have had an impact on her."

Tony frowned. "It didn't help, either, that her father told her all kinds of lies about you, likely one of the most prominent Christian men in her life."

Nick nodded. "It's up to us to show her what true Christian love looks like. Then who knows where things might lead?"

Tony gave his brother a stern sideways glance. He didn't need to be a mind reader to know the direction his brother's thoughts had taken. "They're certainly not going to lead where you're thinking."

"Why not? She's a pretty girl. You guys have always had a good friendship."

He narrowed his eyes. "She has a kid."

"What does that have to do with anything? You love kids."

"You know the answer to that."

Nick planted both fists on his hips. "I know *your* answer, but it's really messed up."

"Hand me that platter." He would put an end to this topic of conversation. "It's time to get these off the grill."

Nick handed him the empty platter with a sigh. It wasn't the first time they'd had this conversation, and it wouldn't be the last.

Tony slid each of the seven steaks from the spatula to the platter and ended with a small hamburger on top for Gavin. Nick walked across the deck ahead of him and swung open one of the French doors leading into the dining room.

The table was already set with seven place settings, complete with china, full silver service and cloth napkins. Two foil-covered casserole dishes sat nestled into metal racks. In the center of the table, three candles rose from a base of fresh greenery.

Although a picnic on paper plates would

have sufficed for his family, with Kris, he didn't expect anything less than the spread before him.

Kris walked into the room carrying a bowl of tossed salad, and his mom and Joanne followed with a variety of salad dressings. Gavin's babysitter slid him into the high chair and sat next to him, and everyone else took their places at the table. Before seating herself, Kris removed the foil from the Pyrex dishes, revealing scalloped potatoes and broccoli casserole.

His father scanned the offerings. "Kris, you outdid yourself."

"With all the work you guys did this afternoon, I owe you a few more dinners like this."

His father gave her a warm smile. "Sweetheart, you don't owe us anything. You didn't even owe us this, although we're going to enjoy it immensely. What we did this afternoon is what friends do for each other."

"Thank you."

There was a catch in her voice. When Tony cast her a sideways glance, she was blinking away moisture. Outside, Nick had mentioned showing her what true Christian love looked like. His dad was an expert.

Being the elder of the group, his father offered a prayer of thanks for the food. Dishes were passed, and everyone settled into easy conversation.

Kris looked around her son to address the babysitter. "Mildred, where are you waiting out the storm?"

"I'm going to my daughter and son-in-law's place. It's farther inland."

Tony's father nodded. "We're doing the same thing. Betty and I are too close to the water, so we're going to wait it out with Nick and Joanne. What about you two?"

"Tony and I are going to my sister's place. Her fiancé works nights for Pensacola PD in patrol and will be on duty, although I'm sure they'll be holed up at the station during the worst of it. Meanwhile, we'll be hunkered down with Kassie and her fiancé's grandmother."

"I'm sure they'll be happy to have you there."

After everyone had had their fill, Kris and Joanne cleared away the plates and almost empty casserole dishes and returned with a stack of small plates, peach cobbler and what looked like homemade whipped cream. Last came a pewter cream and sugar set and two carafes containing coffee, one decaf and one regular, according to Kris.

Oh, man. He should have saved room for dessert.

He was halfway through the tasty treat when a little voice came from the other side of Kris.

"May I be escoosed?"

Kris looked at his plate, which was empty, just like his dinner plate had been. "Sure, sweetie."

Before she could stand, Mildred picked up her napkin and started to wipe his hands. "I'll get him."

When she'd set him on the floor, he

looked up at her with a big smile. "Tank you."

Then he showered Tony with that same smile before running from the room. Something stirred inside. Nick was right. He did like kids. And Gavin was a hard one to not fall in love with.

Some of his good behavior was probably innate—he was just a compliant, easy child. But Tony couldn't discount the excellent parenting he was receiving. If somewhere in the distant future he was ever ready to raise a kid, he hoped it would be one like Gavin.

One by one, each of those gathered finished their dessert and sipped their coffee. As conversation continued, relaxed and natural, a sense of nostalgia settled over him. How many times had he and Nick, along with Mom and Dad, sat around this very table, sharing a meal with the Ashbaughs? Their fathers hadn't just been business partners, they'd been friends.

Sarah Ashbaugh was gone, and Bobby Ashbaugh was in prison, but would the

Sandersons and the other Ashbaughs eventually be able to find their way back into friendship? It looked like it tonight. Even Kris was talkative and relaxed.

Tony leaned back in his chair, full to the point of being almost uncomfortable. If he had Kris cooking for him on a regular basis, he'd have to step up his gym workouts or take up running. In fact, if he had Kris cooking for him, it would be the latter, with her at his side, Gavin in a jogging stroller in front of her. The image he created had a lot of appeal.

The little boy padded back into the room holding a stuffed white rabbit and squeezed between his chair and his mother's. Tony slid back and over, giving him more room.

Instead of climbing into his mother's lap, he turned toward Tony and held out both hands.

Tony swallowed hard, his throat working. He didn't look around the table, but judging from how conversation had come to a sudden stop, every eye was on him, even Mildred's. If he ignored those pleading eyes and outstretched hands, his family would know why. Mildred wouldn't. Neither would Kris.

He slid his hands under Gavin's arms and lifted him onto his lap. The little boy clutched the rabbit against him and snuggled against Tony's chest.

Was the boy trying to make him uncomfortable? Or win him over?

Winning him over wasn't necessary. He'd done that almost right from the start.

Gavin looked up at him and held the rabbit up for inspection. "Bunny."

Tony smiled. "That's a nice bunny. What's his name?"

"'Noball.'"

"Snowball. That's a good name for a white bunny."

"Uh-huh."

Gavin again held the rabbit against his chest and nestled closer to Tony. As conversation around the table resumed, Tony remained ultra-aware of the warm bundle in his lap. Warmth gradually pushed away his nervousness. When he looked at Kris, she was watching him with a soft smile.

Yes, Gavin had won him over, but he wasn't the only one. So had his pretty mother. Could there possibly be a chance for them? If Kris returned to the faith of her childhood and was eventually able to move past the death of her handsome Air Force husband, could they have something much deeper than friendship?

No. How could he even think about getting a ready-made family after Nick and Joanne lost their child while she was in his care? After three miscarriages and losing the one child they'd been able to have, watching him hold Gavin was probably sending a red-hot poker through their hearts.

He shifted his gaze to the opposite side of the table, where Nick sat with his wife. Instead of pain on his brother's face, Tony saw joy. The man was even smiling. So was Joanne.

They'd told him over and over that they didn't blame him. They'd insisted it could have happened with anyone, them included. Maybe they'd really meant it. Maybe someday he'd believe it for himself.

That day hadn't come yet.

Next to him, Kris pushed her chair back. "I'd better work on getting this mess cleaned up so we can all get out of here before dark."

With six of them handling cleanup and Mildred keeping both Bella and Gavin out from underfoot, everything was done in record time.

They moved into the large foyer, with its curved stairway rising to the second floor. At the front door, his dad thanked Kris for the meal and wrapped her in a warm hug. She stiffened for a brief moment before relaxing and returning the hug.

Tony stepped onto the porch first, Nick and Joanne behind him. His parents and Kris followed. Finally, Mildred walked out holding Gavin's hand in hers. The sun had sunk below the horizon, and the final remnants of daylight were barely hanging on.

Tony started down the porch steps toward the curved walk that led to the driveway. His truck sat some twenty feet away, behind Mildred's Camry, Kris's generator in the bed. His parents and Nick and Joanne had ridden together in his dad's F-250, parked on the opposite side of his Tundra.

An explosion rent the silence of the evening, the force knocking him against the porch railing. Behind him, someone screamed. Or maybe it was several someones.

He turned around. Mildred had scooped up Gavin and fled back inside. Kris was following. His father had stepped in front of his mother, as if to shield her with his own body, and Nick had Joanne wrapped in a protective hug.

When he spun back toward the driveway, the front half of his truck was in flames.

"Kris, get me a fire extinguisher."

When he'd arrived, his gas gauge had registered three-quarters. If the tank ignited, it would take out his dad's truck, Mildred's car and possibly Kris's detached garage.

Kris appeared on the porch with a fire extinguisher a half minute later. He didn't need to tell her to call 911. The officers watching the house were driving in their direction and would have already radioed dispatch. More units would be on their way, as would a fire truck.

If the explosion had happened a minute later, an ambulance would have been needed also. Actually, several ambulances.

Thank you, God.

When he got within ten feet of his truck, he pulled the pin on the extinguisher, took aim and squeezed the lever. The stream of dry powder shot from the end of the nozzle. Twenty seconds later, that stream was gone. Fortunately, all that remained of the fire was some smoke.

The unmarked unit drew to a stop at the edge of the road, and the driver exited. "We've already called it in. Are you guys all right?"

"Except for being a little shaken up, we're fine. I just don't understand how someone got close enough to plant a bomb with you guys sitting fifty or sixty feet away."

"It wasn't planted here. You did leave for a short time this afternoon."

The man was right. He'd made his Publix run without giving it a second thought. Big mistake. Police were watching everywhere Kris went. They weren't watching him. Although he hadn't been in the store more than fifteen minutes, it had been enough time for someone to attach a bomb to his truck.

Kris moved up next to him. She'd apparently left Gavin inside with Mildred. "As soon as Mark's parents get back, I'm heading for Ohio."

She'd already let him know they'd responded to her message. She was welcome and could stay as long as she liked.

"That's a good idea." It was what he'd wanted her to do all along.

"You could have been killed. So could

your parents and brother and sister-in-law." She shifted her gaze to the officer who had joined them. "As much as I want to make it easier for you to catch this guy, my presence is putting people I care about in danger. I can't stay."

Tony nodded. He was thinking about her while she was thinking about others. The reasons for her leaving didn't matter.

As long as they could keep her location a secret from the killer, she'd be safe.

That fact just about made it worth losing his truck.

SEVEN

The wind howled and rain beat against the roof and the plywood covering the windows. Around the room, several candles flickered from places well out of the reach of Bella's tail or nose. They'd lost power an hour ago. Already, the house was getting stuffy.

Although it was nearing midnight, Kris was too wound up to feel sleepy. The threat to her dog, the bomb planted under Tony's truck and now the storm hammering them—it was almost enough to make her want to beg for help from the God she hadn't spoken to since learning of Mark's death.

According to Tony, a security camera near the charter office had captured a boy of about ten or twelve setting the box containing the shredded stuffed animal in front of the neighboring store, but none of the cameras had picked up whoever had passed it off to him to begin with. This morning, Tony had gotten a rental and was still waiting to hear whether his truck would be declared a total loss. The preliminary investigation had determined that a homemade bomb had been taped to the Tundra's engine splash guard and remote detonated as they walked out the door.

What wasn't determined was whether the killer was just issuing a warning or whether he'd planned to blow up the car with Tony, Gavin and her inside. If the latter, maybe he'd changed his mind when he'd seen that two other couples would likely be collateral damage.

Kassie rose and walked to the double window, now covered with plywood. She didn't look any more relaxed than Kris felt. Neither did Tony. Even Ms. MaryAnn, Jared's grandmother, was wide awake.

Only Gavin was oblivious to the storm raging outside. Around ten, Kassie had made him a bed of blankets in the corner. He'd snuggled with Snowball and gone promptly to sleep. Kris envied him. She wasn't likely to sleep soundly again until she got to her in-laws' house late Saturday night. Leaving somehow felt like letting the killer win, but last night's attack was the final straw.

Kassie cupped her hands on either side of her face and peered through a small cutout in the plywood.

"See anything?" Kris asked.

"Nothing except a river flowing over the Plexiglas."

Tony shook his head. "I can't believe you have windows in your plywood."

"That wasn't my doing. The prior owners had an overly curious twelve-year-old that kept wanting to peek out the front door during Michael. So the dad cut an eight-by-ten opening in a couple of the larger sheets and screwed Plexiglas against them."

She walked back to the chair she'd been sitting in. "It would probably be a great idea if it wasn't pitch black out there and the wind wasn't throwing solid sheets of rain against the front of the house."

A muffled crash sounded from the back, and Kassie jumped. "I hope that was just a limb and not the whole tree."

Kris winced. A huge oak tree stood in the backyard about twenty feet from the bedrooms. If one of the larger limbs hit the house, the roof would likely have extensive damage. If the whole tree came down, it could take out the back half of the house.

Kassie picked up the flashlight she'd put on the coffee table before the power had gone out.

Tony rose, too. "I'll follow you."

Kris gave Ms. MaryAnn an uneasy smile. "I think it's going to be a long night."

"It is. But this isn't my first rodeo." She returned Kris's tight smile with one much more relaxed. The woman had a sense of peace about her that was at odds with the storm raging outside. "Jared put plywood on the windows, and we secured everything the best we could. The rest is up to the Lord. Of course, Jared and I prayed for protection over the house before he headed to the station and I came over here."

"If you want to extend some of those prayers to include this place and my house on Bayou Texar, we won't complain."

"We're already praying for protection here, but I'll be happy to include your place, too."

Kris waited for the mini sermon, but it didn't come. According to Kassie, Ms. MaryAnn was instrumental in getting her back into church, which led to her renewing the commitment she'd made as a child. But maybe preaching at her wasn't Ms. MaryAnn's style.

"Thank you for the prayers." Though she appreciated them, she didn't have near the confidence in them that Ms. MaryAnn seemed to have. Her own peace of mind came from good, solid storm shutters. And insurance.

The wind intensified, the howl becoming a roar. Gavin hugged his stuffed rabbit more tightly and released a sigh without waking up. The eye wall of the storm was supposed to pass about forty miles west of them. The fact they weren't getting the eye directly wasn't much consolation. The winds on the right side of the storm were always the strongest.

She frowned at Jared's grandmother. "Jared isn't out in this, is he?"

Ms. MaryAnn shook her head. "They're waiting it out at the station. As soon as it's safe to venture out, they'll be ready to respond to emergencies." She paused. "I don't know when his shift will actually end. I think it'll be all hands on deck for a while. Besides other emergencies, with power out and businesses shut down, there's always the concern about looting. But he'll make it home eventually."

Kris nodded. "Home" for Jared was currently with his grandmother. He'd moved in four months ago when she'd returned home after finishing rehab for a broken hip.

Now she was fully recovered, or close to it. In fact, she was already looking forward to getting back out on the pickleball court, which was how she'd broken her hip to begin with.

Jared was still there, without any immediate plans to leave. During his grandmother's convalescent period, he'd gotten to know Kassie and had fallen in love. Now he wasn't in any hurry to return to his home in nearby Nice. Ms. MaryAnn didn't seem to be anxious to throw him out, either.

Kris cast a glance toward the hallway. What was taking Kassie and Tony so long? Any discussion they might be having wasn't penetrating the howling of the storm outside. As much as she wanted to know how Kassie's house was faring, she didn't want to leave her son or Jared's grandmother to find out.

Finally, Kassie walked back into the room and laid the flashlight on the table.

Tony was right behind her. "There's no water coming in, not yet, anyway. No drips, no wetness on the ceiling as far as we can tell."

Kassie eased down on the couch next to Kris. "Thank the Lord, it looks like we dodged a bullet on that one."

Kris pursed her lips. "I hope mine is also faring well."

Tony eased down on her other side and gave her a casual sideways hug. "With those hurricane shutters we all installed, it should breeze through this."

Yeah, he was right. Her house was as protected as it could possibly be, thanks to Tony and his family. They'd worked so hard, sacrificing their time for her when they'd obviously had their own homes to secure. They'd made it fun, too. The friction that had always characterized the Ashbaugh relationships had somehow bypassed the Sandersons.

It had all made for a really emotional

day. The love and acceptance she'd experienced from the people she'd so long viewed as her enemies had put her on the verge of tears more than once. Even more unexpected was the longing that had risen up at odd times—the desire to be a part of this family. She wasn't naïve enough to believe the Sandersons were perfect, but compared to the Ashbaughs, they weren't far from it.

And then there was Tony. Learning what had really happened all those years ago, finding out that he had valued her friendship as much as she had valued his, had made it hard to hang on to her heart. But how could she give her heart to Tony when it still belonged to Mark? Tony deserved better than that. Gavin did, too. Tony was making headway—he was a lot more comfortable around him than he'd been at first. But her little boy deserved to have someone who was all-in.

She shook off the impractical thoughts. She and Tony would never be more than friends. The dream of becoming a part of his family was nothing but a fantasy. She had no doubt Tony cared for her. But he hadn't given her a single hint that he was interested in anything more than friendship, or that he was even attracted to her. Hugs had been for the sole purpose of providing comfort. That fierce sense of protectiveness he displayed was nothing more than he'd feel for any other woman, both as a cop and as a man.

She would never belong to the Sanderson family, but maybe she could eventually be a part of one just like it.

Tony took his arm from around her shoulders and leaned against her to pull his phone from his pants pocket. She watched his fingers slide across the screen.

How you guys faring?

The contact name across the top was Nick Sanderson. Yep, Tony backed up what she'd just been thinking. Instead of viewing everything in life as a competition, Tony and Nick cheered each other on, celebrating each other's accomplishments.

She and Kassie were slowly getting there. It had only taken them twenty-seven years. But when it came to Alyssa, they were still nowhere close.

She wouldn't be getting a text or phone call from Alyssa tonight. She was likely too wrapped up in her own problems to think about checking on her older sisters who were in the middle of a Cat. 4 hurricane.

Tony's phone buzzed with a reply.

Good so far. You?

Something hit house but seems OK.

Prayers.

Same here.

Yeah that was a conversation she and Alyssa would have…like never.

Kris's phone started to ring from its place on the end table, and she lifted her eyebrows. Maybe she'd been thinking bad thoughts about her younger sister unjustly. She rose and snatched up the phone. Alyssa's name wasn't displayed. Instead, the screen showed Blocked.

That didn't mean anything. It could still be Alyssa. Maybe she'd had to have her number changed and was having to lie low. Kris wouldn't be surprised. Whenever Alyssa found her way out of trouble, it didn't take her long to find her way back in.

Kris crossed the room and swiped to accept the call. The gravely voice on the other end of the line definitely wasn't Alyssa's.

"I was going to make it fast, but you've ticked me off. Now you'll go like the others."

Her breath hitched, and she stood frozen for several moments. Finally, she found her voice. "Who is this?"

Silence. She was speaking to dead air.

"Kris?" Tony rose and crossed the room. All other eyes were on her, too.

She slowly lowered the phone. "It was the killer. He said he'd planned to kill me fast, but now he's going to make me go like the others."

She shuddered at the image that flashed into her mind and stuck there in glaring detail—dark brown hair matted with dried blood, skull smashed in, bits of bone and tissue protruding. She shook her head to try to clear the image. It didn't help. Tony stepped closer and drew her into his arms. She slid her own around his waist, surrendering to the comfort and protection he offered.

When they'd found the body in the woods, he'd put one arm around her and pressed her against his side. The night of Shannon's murder, he'd reached into the truck to squeeze her shoulder, as he had on several occasions since.

This was different. Now he stood with both arms wrapped around her, squeezing her against him, the side of her face pressed against his chest. It had been eighteen long months since a man had held her like that, and tears rose up from some unknown place to sting her eyes. She would let him be her rock, however temporary that might be.

She spoke into his shirt. "My number was in Shannon's phone. He's been hanging on to it all this time."

Tony rested his chin on the top of her head, making her feel even more cocooned. She drew in a deep breath and released it slowly, allowing the tension to drain from her body.

"In a little over twenty-four hours, you'll be on your way to Ohio. In the meantime, I'm not going to let you out of my sight."

She closed her eyes. Soon she'd be gone, far away from Pensacola and all its threats.

Far away from her family. Far away from Tony.

Safety was requiring too much sacrifice.

How long would it be before she'd get her life back? Sometimes serial killers escaped justice for years. Some were never caught.

Would it ever be safe for her to return home?

And what about her relationship with Tony? After dinner last night, Gavin had climbed into his lap, and he didn't look ready to bolt from the room. He'd seemed to relax, had even wrapped an arm around her little boy.

How long would it take for Gavin to weave his way into Tony's heart so thoroughly that that "package deal" would be exactly what he wanted? And how long would it take for her to let go of everything she had with Mark and love again?

If she could stay, would there be a chance for Tony and her?

Maybe she would never know.

Yes, safety was requiring far too much sacrifice.

Kris stepped over a downed tree limb and made her way through the thick carpet of twigs and leaves that covered Kassie's yard. Tony walked next to her, Kassie a short distance ahead. A large limb lay on the roof, the source of the crash they'd heard last night. Other smaller ones were scattered about the asphalt shingles.

The power was still out. It likely wouldn't be restored for several days, much longer in outlying areas.

Kassie peered up with a frown. "That probably did some damage, but I'm guessing it's just surface. If it had put a hole in the roof decking, I'd have some major water stains in my spare bedroom."

Tony nodded. "I'll try to get up there today to clean off the roof and see what we have."

"If we need to tarp it, I've got a couple in the garage."

That would be a common sight for the next few months—neighborhoods a patchwork of blue tarps.

Tony continued. "Let's check the rest of the house. Then we'll see how Ms. Mary-Ann's place fared."

They'd left her inside with Gavin. She'd

agreed that she didn't need to be traipsing through an obstacle course so soon after recovering from a broken hip. She'd already announced her plans for a long nap as soon as she could safely return home.

When they'd all finally gone to bed at three in the morning, the outer bands had still been battering them. Kris had carried Gavin with her to the spare bedroom, Tony had stretched out on the couch and Ms. MaryAnn had insisted she'd be quite comfortable in the recliner.

Those nap plans Ms. MaryAnn had mentioned had a lot of appeal. Maybe Kris would be able to squeeze one in herself this afternoon. Making a drive from Florida to Ohio in her sleep-deprived state didn't seem much safer than staying where there was a killer after her.

When they'd finished circling the house, Kassie crossed her arms. "I know how I'll be spending my day. It'll take hours to haul the limbs to the road and rake the yard. Then I'll see how much cleanup I can do next door by the time Jared gets home."

That would be another common sight— huge piles of yard debris stacked along the road until the authorities could haul it all away.

Kassie continued. "But first, the ply-wood has to go so I can open the windows. We'll want to get the generator hooked up, too."

Since it had been in the bed of his truck and the explosion had just impacted the front, the generator had survived. It wasn't powerful enough to run the air condi-tioner, but they could keep their phones charged and have lights. The refrigerator and freezer would work, too.

Tony looked at Kassie. "I'll do what I can, until I get called in, anyway." He shifted his gaze to Kris. "Once we get the plywood down and the generator going, we'll check your place."

An ache formed in her stomach at the thought. Homes right on the water almost always fared worse in hurricanes.

At least her protection detail was back on this morning. She'd been relieved to see the SUV when she'd peered out the front door upon getting up.

Tony held out a hand. "Let's check your neighbor's place. I'm sure she's anxiously awaiting word."

Jared's grandmother's yard looked much the same as Kassie's—buried beneath a blanket of limbs, twigs and leaves. The house itself was fine. Even the shed out back was untouched. Maybe the prayers the older lady had sent up had done some good. Hopefully, they'd worked for the Ashbaugh family home, too.

Kassie fell into step beside Kris. "What do you say we have Tony hook up the generator, and while he's taking down plywood, we can whip up some scrambled eggs and sausage for this hungry bunch?"

"That sounds good."

"We'll need to check the charter office building, too."

Kris followed her into the house while Tony headed to the garage to get them

some temporary power. If the office building sustained damage, Kassie would be
dealing with it alone, on top of handling
the operations of the charter business and
keeping Kassie's Kuts running smoothly.

Kris pulled the door shut behind them.
This was the worst possible time for her
to bail. If she had another option, she'd
take it.

Ms. MaryAnn looked up from the book
she'd been reading to Gavin. He sat in her
lap, Snowball clutched against his chest.

"How bad is it?"

"Not bad at all," Kassie said. "Everything's a mess, but it doesn't look like
there are repairs to make beyond some
possible missing or damaged shingles. Tony's hooking up the generator so we've got
lights and refrigeration, and we're going to
make some breakfast on the camp stove."

"Good. Your little one here has been
saying he's hungry. I told him his mommy
and auntie would be back inside in a few
minutes."

She returned to her reading. It was a

story about Noah's ark. Kassie had several Bible stories mixed in with the popular fairytales, and when given a choice, those were what she usually read to him.

Kris didn't mind. Despite her own lack of faith, she had no problem with her sister teaching him about God. Even though she'd turned her back on God, she couldn't get away from the feeling that she'd be shortchanging her little boy if she didn't at least expose him to Christianity so when he got older, he could make an informed choice.

But she had time. Bringing him to church wasn't that important at his age. Or maybe it was.

She and Kassie had just started breakfast preparations when most of the lights in the front of the house came on.

"Woo-hoo!" Kassie gave her a big grin. "We've got power. Since the AC isn't kicking on, I'm guessing we've got Tony to thank rather than Florida Power."

While waiting for the sausage patties to

brown, Kris glanced into the living room. Tony was right outside the front window, judging from the whine of the screw gun. The plywood shifted, and glove-covered fingers wrapped around the top and bottom.

When he'd set the large sheet aside, he smiled at her through the glass. She gave him a friendly wave, and her heart made a little flip. Fortunately, he couldn't see the latter. She needed to get a grip. Finding out she'd had a crush on him in high school had probably been uncomfortable enough for him. If he had an inkling of the feelings she was struggling with now, awkward wouldn't begin to describe the experience.

Maybe she was being too hard on herself. With everything she'd been through the past year and a half, it was no wonder her emotions were all over the place. Once she was out of danger and got settled back into her old life, she'd regain the control she craved.

She and Kris had just finished the eggs and sausage when the front door creaked open.

Tony stepped into the kitchen. "That's it. The windows are all uncovered, and the pieces of plywood are stored back in your garage."

Kassie carried a stack of paper plates and plastic cups to the table. "Perfect timing. Breakfast is ready. I don't entertain like my sister does." She plunked two cartons on the table—one of milk and one of orange juice—next to a carafe of coffee. "Especially right after a hurricane."

"Hey, as long as there's plenty and it tastes good, I'm happy. Based on what I'm looking at and how it smells, you succeeded on both counts."

The food had just been blessed and passed when Kris's phone buzzed with a text. She'd left it charging on the kitchen counter. It was probably someone checking to see how they'd weathered the storm. They could wait until she'd eaten.

She refused to entertain the other possibility, that the killer was making another threat, this one by text.

Tony's buzzed a few seconds later, and he pulled it from his pocket. "Uh-oh."

"What?"

"A mobile home park got hit hard. Apparently the storm spawned a tornado. A lot of the homes are flattened. Not everyone evacuated."

"We're doing a search and rescue operation?"

He narrowed his eyes at her. "There's no *we* to it."

Her heart kicked into high gear. She always felt a bit of an adrenaline rush when she got those notifications. Even more so now.

"Your guys can watch me there just as well as here or at the charter office. Even more so. The place will be crawling with law enforcement and rescue workers."

"Don't even think about it."

"This is likely your last shot at trying to catch this guy when you have an inclination of when and where he might strike."

And if they were successful in apprehending him today, she wouldn't have to flee her home.

Tony was quiet. Whether he was considering her words or thinking of ways to strengthen his argument, she wasn't sure.

"Look, if I leave, there's no guarantee that he won't somehow find me. The only way I'll truly be safe is for you guys to get him off the street."

She looked at her sister. "Kassie, tell him I'm right. I can't leave you to handle everything on your own. I need to make this one last-ditch effort to ensure my safety and preserve your sanity."

Kassie held up both hands. "Don't involve me in this. I totally get where you're coming from, but I can see Tony's point, too."

Kris shifted her gaze to Ms. MaryAnn. She'd take an ally wherever she could get one.

The older woman shook her head. "I'm not touching this one."

Tony heaved a sigh. "I'm not saying yes,

but I'm not saying no, either. I'll talk to those in charge and see how they want this to go down.

"Good."

All she could do was wait and see. Without the blessing of the police, she wouldn't even attempt it, no matter how many rescue workers were around.

Not even with Tony at her side.

EIGHT

Tony eased the Nissan Rogue to a stop at a darkened traffic light, Kris in the passenger seat beside him and Bella in the back. Gavin had stayed behind with Ms. MaryAnn. Tony hadn't received word yet on the fate of his Tundra. In the meantime, the rental wasn't a bad ride.

After waiting for a vehicle to pass in front of him, he looked both ways before creeping through himself. With no working traffic lights in town, every intersection was being treated as a four-way stop.

He glanced in his rearview mirror. The vehicle that had been parked in front of Kassie's this morning was framed there. It would stay with them throughout the day. Kassie was behind it, waiting to get through the same intersection they'd both just cleared.

The dark traffic lights weren't the only sign of the storm that had ravaged the area last night. Signs in front of businesses had been blown out, leaving only the frames. The wind had lifted several carport roofs, curling them back over houses or tearing them completely off and depositing them some distance away.

They'd only gone a few blocks but had already passed two houses split almost in half by huge uprooted oak trees. Road crews had come through and cleared the main streets, but debris covered the parking lots, driveways and yards.

He glanced over at Kris. Her eyebrows were drawn together, forming vertical creases between them. The view outside the SUV's windows wasn't doing anything to alleviate that concern.

He still hadn't apologized to her for snapping at her a couple of nights ago. He should have done it right away, but there'd been the situation with the box.

The next day, they'd been busy with hurricane prep. Yesterday, he'd worked his shift, and they'd gone straight to Kassie's.

He drew in a stabilizing breath. He needed to tell her he was sorry, and putting it off wasn't going to make it any easier.

"I owe you an apology."

She didn't respond. When he cast her a sideways glance, she was staring out the front windshield, waiting for him to continue.

"You were right that something happened. You asked me what it was, and I didn't want to talk about it." He still didn't.

She crossed her arms. "I would say I shouldn't have pushed, but I didn't push. I just offered a listening ear."

"I know you did, and I was wrong. I shouldn't have snapped at you."

He turned onto Yates. It hadn't been cleared like the main roads. Small limbs and twigs crunched beneath his tires as he proceeded toward Kris's street. He weaved around a large tree limb that someone had pulled toward the edge of the road.

Kris sat in silence. He did, too. But he wasn't finished, not by a long shot. He just couldn't seem to find the words.

She uncrossed her arms and let her hands rest in her lap. "You know all about my dysfunctional family. You were there when my mom took off. That was ten years ago. In all that time, none of us have gotten so much as a postcard. She embraced her new life and made a clean break with the old, even though that old life included three devastated daughters. And you know that messed-up younger sister I have? She's twenty-five and still hasn't gotten her life straightened out. And then there's my dad. He wasn't just an alcoholic. He was also a drug runner."

She heaved a sigh and let her head rest against the seat. "I know we're just friends, and that's all we'll ever be, but even friends share with one another."

"I know." He didn't acknowledge her statement that they'd never be more than friends, or the unexpected stab of pain that shot through him with the thought. He couldn't tell her how he felt, that he was dangerously close to falling in love with her. The confession would serve no purpose. He wasn't the father her little boy needed, but someone out there was. Both Kris and Gavin deserved that chance for happiness.

He crept down the road, glad for the distraction of driving. If he didn't have to look at Kris while he told his story, he wouldn't have to see the judgment in her eyes.

"June, a year ago, Nick and Joanne took a weekend trip for their anniversary. They left me to take care of their ten-month-old daughter. I put her to bed and went in to check on her a short time later. She was sleeping peacefully. I turned on the TV, watched a movie. When it was over, I wanted to check on her once more before heading to bed myself."

He tightened his fingers around the steering wheel as unwanted images crashed into his mind. After drawing in a stabilizing breath, he continued.

"I opened her door and tiptoed into her room. I could barely see her in the light coming in from the hallway. She was lying on her back, the way I had left her, her face turned toward me. But something didn't look right."

"Oh, no." She whispered the words. She'd already figured out where the story was heading.

"Her stomach wasn't rising and falling, and even in the poor lighting, her color-ing looked wrong." Or maybe that part had been his imagination, fear taking over. "I turned on the bedside lamp, and her lips had a bluish tint. Her ears did, too. I checked, and she definitely wasn't breath-ing."

The events that followed played through his mind, almost immobilizing him. A warm hand settled over his, still grip-ping the wheel. The touch gave him the strength to continue.

"I tried to revive her. I dialed 911, put

the dispatcher on speaker phone and continued to work on Zoe through the whole conversation. Nothing I did worked."

Not even prayer. Granted, his prayers weren't eloquent. They were nothing but *God, please* over and over. He didn't know whether Nick and Joanne had ever asked why, but *he* certainly had.

He stopped in Kris's driveway. The unmarked vehicle following them parked at the edge of the road, and Kassie pulled in behind the Nissan. Except for the debris scattered around it, the house looked much the same as it had when he'd left it two days ago. If there was damage, it was most likely in the back.

He killed the Rogue's engine and let his hands fall to his lap. "If only I would have checked on her sooner. I waited the entire length of the movie."

He turned his head until his gaze met hers, steeling himself for the blame he expected to see. There wasn't any. Instead, sympathy and understanding filled her eyes.

She shook her head. "You had already checked on her, and she was fine. This could have happened at any time. She could have stopped breathing when you were sound asleep."

"But she didn't. This happened on my watch. If I would have checked on her sooner, I might have been able to save her. Or if I had decided to read instead of watch TV, I might have heard something. This is all on me. That's why I've vowed to never again be responsible for someone else's child." Maybe he shouldn't even be responsible for his own.

Her face fell. Was it from the realization that they could never be together? Or was what happened a non-issue because she wasn't interested in anything more than friendship anyway?

She spoke softly. "Do Nick and Joanne blame you?"

"They never have. They've insisted that the outcome probably wouldn't have been any different if they'd been there."

No, his brother and sister-in-law didn't

blame him, but he'd never been able to stop blaming himself. How would he ever move past the trauma of holding his dead niece in his arms?

"They're right, you know. Sudden infant death syndrome has taken countless babies' lives. This wasn't your fault. You can't keep living under a burden of guilt that isn't yours to carry."

She again rested her hand on his, this time sliding her fingers into his palm. Her reassuring squeeze conveyed her acceptance. It was like salve on the tattered pieces of his heart.

"Thank you." He returned the squeeze. He appreciated the thought, but it didn't change anything. He had let his niece die while he'd been watching TV thirty feet from where she'd been sleeping.

He forced a small smile. "Are you ready to check out your place?"

"As ready as I'll ever be."

They stepped from the SUV, and Kassie met Kris at the passenger door.

"It's still standing, so that's a good sign."

Kris opened the back door, and Bella jumped out. Not only was the house still standing, but viewed from the front, there wasn't any obvious damage. They'd know for sure once they checked the upstairs for water intrusion and walked around back.

Kris unclipped her keys from her purse and made her way toward the front door, Kassie following. Tony trailed behind. There was a sidewalk under him somewhere, hidden beneath all the leaves and twigs that had blown from the trees.

The flowering plants and other ornamentals he'd admired on prior visits were buried also. He'd make it a point to get over here as soon as possible and see what he could salvage of all her hard work.

When Kris opened the front door, Bella was the first one inside, clearly excited to be home. After a quick tour of the first floor, Kris hurried up the stairs and into her bedroom. It looked the same as it had the last time he'd walked in, minus Gavin's crib, which he'd disassembled and taken to the office.

Tony looked up at the ceiling, something he hadn't done the last time he'd been here. "It looks like you have some staining."

Kris nodded. "That was from Michael. We ended up getting the roof reshingled, courtesy of the insurance company. We just never got around to hitting the ceilings with a stain blocker."

She frowned. "After this much time, there's probably no excuse. For the past several years, Dad had been dealing with his issues and sort of let the place go. And since I moved in here a year and a half ago, any repairs beyond the urgent just haven't been high on my priority list."

She led them into the two spare bedrooms and finally the large room at the other end. Judging from the masculine furnishings and the appearance of having been untouched for months, it had likely been her father's room.

Each of the rooms along the back had the same staining, which Kris insisted hadn't changed. Apparently, the roof had held up well.

Kris led them toward the stairs. Upon a closer look, it wasn't just the ceiling that needed attention. The hardwood floor needed buffing and waxing, and the walls could do with a fresh coat of paint.

Maybe he could announce a Sanderson work day. He didn't even have to get the go-ahead from his father or brother. They'd be on board. So would his mom and Joanne.

Except Kris might not appreciate being their project. She'd accepted help with hurricane prep. She'd had no choice. Aside from the fact that someone was trying to kill her, she would never have been able to handle all those shutters by herself, especially on the second-floor windows.

But this was different. There was no nature-imposed deadline. She would insist that she could handle it, that she'd get to it eventually. He could be just as insistent.

When they exited and circled the house, the side and back looked much the same as the front.

Tony picked up a two-foot-by-three-foot

piece of thin plywood, its edges weathered and rotting. One side was painted white, and an oval hole had been cut out, with a screen stapled over the opening

He held up the piece. "Looks like you lost some soffit."

Inspection of the eaves confirmed his suspicions. Judging from the voids, more than one piece had come down.

He turned around and looked toward the water, past a large cypress tree. "Oh, man, your gazebo is flattened."

Kris followed his gaze, and hardness entered hers. "Good riddance. I've always hated that thing anyway."

At his lifted brows, she continued. "My dad had it built right after my mom left, like a monument to her infidelity."

He stepped to the side to gain a clearer view of that part of the shoreline. Boards were strewn along the beach, with railings and sections of roof mixed in. The floor had even been lifted from its supports and lay much closer to the water than he remembered.

Something else was there, too, protruding from the sand. Something that didn't look like wood or any kind of construction material.

Without offering an explanation, he walked toward the water's edge. Three of the gazebo's support posts were still embedded in the ground. The other three were missing, washed somewhere down the beach or out into the bayou.

But it was what was in the center of those remaining posts that had snagged his gaze and held it.

Bones.

Were they human? He couldn't be sure, but they looked a lot like a femur and the two smaller bones in the lower leg.

A soft gasp behind him was the first indication that someone had followed him. Kassie and Kris stood side by side, eyes wide. Each had a hand covering her mouth.

Bella shot past them and started to dig. Tony sprang toward the dog, but before he could reach her, Kris's voice cut through his panic. "Bella, come."

Her tone was commanding, with a mild sternness. The dog obeyed immediately, trotted to her and sat down at her side.

He looked back at the find on the beach. Bella had unearthed some smaller bones. Without poking around, he couldn't say for sure, but if he had to guess, he'd say he was looking at part of a human hand.

He pulled his phone from his pocket. "We need to call the authorities. This will need to be preserved and properly investigated."

Kassie looked at Kris. "Do you think Dad knew someone was buried here?"

Kris shook her head. "I don't know. Maybe he didn't. Maybe it was coincidental that that's the spot he picked to build the gazebo."

Kassie gave her the same *get real* look she used to give her when they'd argued as teenagers.

But Kris wasn't that naïve. The lack of conviction in her tone said she didn't believe her words any more than he and Kassie did.

He had questions of his own, beyond *Did he know?* What he really wanted to find out was whether Ashbaugh had anything to do with disposing of the body, or even more importantly, whether the death had happened by his hand.

Maybe the biggest question of all was whose bones were they? Did those bones have anything to do with their mother's disappearance? Neither Kassie nor Kris was ready for a bombshell like that.

He'd known about their mother leaving and how it had affected each one of the girls. He'd been there to see the devastation. Their father had retreated into the bottle and never found his way out. Kassie had cried for weeks on end. Kris's pain had rapidly turned into hatred. Alyssa had simply gone off the deep end.

Identifying the bones would take time, but he was confident what they would reveal. Learning their mother didn't leave them by choice would be good for Kris, but finding out her father likely killed her and hid her body under the gazebo would shatter her. Whatever the outcome, he'd be there for her.

Kris spun away from the gazebo's remains. "We'll let the authorities handle it."

As she stalked toward the house, Bella trotted behind her, and Tony fell in next to her. Her jaw was set in determination. Whether it was a refusal to believe her father could have done the unthinkable or a determination to be strong whatever the outcome, he wasn't sure.

She'd always been close to the man, had even seemed to put him on a pedestal. Watching him fall from that position of honor in her thoughts to a lowly criminal had to have devastated her.

Kassie trailed behind them, not attempting to engage her sister in conversation. He and Kassie had both spent enough time with her to know better than to try to talk to her when she was upset. Even a comforting hug wouldn't be well received right now, no matter how badly he wanted to give it.

She rounded the corner of the house and headed for the front door, key ready. "I'm locking up. My phone's in my purse, but it's probably time to be heading out."

Tony frowned. He'd rather she not remind him. As much as he didn't like it, Kris was right. Allowing her to participate in the search and rescue operation, under the watchful eye of the Pensacola Police Department, was their last best chance to catch this guy.

Everyone else had agreed, too. Besides the unmarked unit currently waiting beside the road, several other law enforcement officers would be on site in plain clothes, spread throughout the park, keeping watch while they blended in with the rescue workers.

God, please give us a break.

He wanted to catch this guy in the worst way. He just didn't want to put Kris in jeopardy in the process.

And please protect Kris while we try to do this.

* * *

Bella picked her way up a haphazard mountain of wallboard, studs, pipes, insulation, electrical wiring and broken glass while Kris waited on the ground a few yards away.

The dog was working off leash. Based on the excitement rippling through her body, someone was buried somewhere in the hodgepodge of building materials that used to be a double-wide mobile home.

Tony stood with Kris, watching Bella move across the pile, alternating looking down and lifting her head to sniff the air.

Suddenly, the dog stopped, stood stock still, then sat.

Tony leaned toward Kris. "What's she doing?"

"She just alerted." Kris's pulse kicked into high gear, and she hollered at a rescue worker standing in front of a home catty-corner from them. "We've got someone over here."

The man hurried toward them, speaking into his radio as he walked. Within a minute, two others had joined him.

Kris turned away to head down the street. As much as she'd love to see the fruit of Bella's labor and actually witness the rescue, the two of them still had work to do.

There were two more damaged homes to check on her assigned street. The residents of both had told the manager of the park that they would evacuate, so those homes had been assigned a lower priority and left till last.

Those evacuation plans weren't always a sure thing, though. The resident of the home they'd just left had done the same thing and then apparently changed their mind. He or she was likely regretting the decision.

Kris walked down the street toward another collapsed home. The damage to the park was clearly the work of a tornado. It had touched down at one edge and then cut a jagged path through the center, leaving some homes untouched and others completely demolished.

The place they'd just left had been Bella's second find of the day. The first one had happened just before lunchtime. The dog had worked tirelessly since they'd arrived—seven straight hours with a couple of short breaks.

With plenty of workers wandering around the park, Tony's primary job had been protecting her. So far, his protection hadn't been needed. There'd been no sign of the killer or anyone who looked at all suspicious.

It made sense. To attack her when she was surrounded by so many people, the man would have to be insane. Or incredibly bold.

She'd been hoping for the latter. After succeeding several times, killers sometimes got overconfident and took reckless chances just for the thrill of it. It was often those reckless chances that gave the authorities the breaks they needed to catch the guys.

So far, that wasn't happening. It was late afternoon, and the search was drawing to a close. The slim chance that she wasn't going to have to leave for Ohio early tomorrow morning had gotten even slimmer.

The search for survivors in the wreckage of the last two homes didn't take long. No one was there. She headed back toward the Nissan, which Tony had parked at the end of the next street over. He walked next to her, his T-shirt spotted with perspiration and the radio he'd carried all day attached to the waistband of his jeans.

He pulled the keys from his pocket but was too far away to use the fob. "Any ideas for dinner?"

"Not a clue."

"I vote for takeout."

"Sounds like a plan." The last thing she felt like doing was cooking. "I need to go back by the house so I can get packed for my trip north."

"We'll need to make it fast. I want to get

you inside your sister's house well before dark."

She frowned. "I'll do my best."

Gathering their things together for the stay above the charter office had been a breeze. But how would she even begin to pack for an out-of-state trip with no idea of how long she'd be gone?

When they reached the end of the road, they rounded the corner. The Nissan sat in the distance. A boy of about twelve or thirteen barreled toward them, with one of the men who'd been watching the charter office about twenty feet behind him.

Tony sidestepped, his arms shooting out to grab the kid. As the boy veered around him, Tony extended his foot. The kid went briefly airborne before crashing to the asphalt. Tony dropped to his knees next to him and grasped his arms before he could rise and take off again.

The man who had been chasing him closed the gap between them, breathing heavily. "He put something on the windshield of the Nissan, an envelope or piece of paper. When he saw us approaching, he ran."

Tony pulled the kid to his feet, and he made a futile attempt to twist away. "Let me go."

"Not yet. First, we're going to see what you left for us."

Keeping a firm grip on the boy's wrist, Tony led them to the rental vehicle. A sheet of paper was folded in thirds and tucked under one of the wiper blades. Tony removed it, handling it much more carefully than the kid probably had.

After passing the boy off to the other man, he unfolded the sheet, touching just the corners. Kris craned her neck, but couldn't read what was there.

Tony skimmed the page, and his features darkened. "Did you write this?"

"No. I don't even know what it is." He looked from Tony to the other man. "Are you guys cops or something?"

Neither of them answered the question.

The kid tried again to jerk his arm free. "Look, I didn't do anything wrong."

"Then why did you run?"

"The guy who gave me this said to make sure no one saw me."

"What guy was that?"

"I don't know who he was."

"What did he look like?"

The kid's gaze shifted to the side. "I didn't pay any attention."

"What was he driving?"

"I didn't pay any attention to that, either."

Tony continued as if he didn't notice the obvious signs the boy was lying. "Where did you meet this guy?"

"On the road that runs in front of the mobile home park."

"So, he gave you the note. Then what?"

"He said he'd give me twenty bucks if I put it on your windshield."

"Anything you can tell us that will help us find this guy?"

"Uh-uh."

"What's your name?"

"Noah."

Tony bent at the waist, putting him almost eye level with the kid. "Let me tell you something, Noah. We *are* cops. The note you delivered threatens this lady's life. That puts you in a lot of trouble, so you'd better start talking. What did the guy look like?"

He hesitated only a moment longer. "He had blond hair, a little past his shoulders, and a beard and mustache."

Tony straightened. "How about his vehicle?"

"He got out of a car."

"Not a pickup truck?"

"No, definitely a car."

"What kind?"

"I don't know."

Tony narrowed his eyes.

"I'm telling you the truth. It was silver, or more like gray, because it wasn't shiny. It looked older. But I don't know what kind it was."

"Two-door or four-door?"

"Four-door."

Tony looked at the other man. "How about calling it in? He's probably long gone, but we know we're looking for an older gray sedan. Same suspect."

While the other man spoke into his radio, Tony shifted his attention back to the kid. "Anything else you noticed?"

Noah shook his head. "Don't tell him I told you. He looks really strong. If he found me and knew I told, I think he'd hurt me."

"It'll be our little secret."

Kris watched Noah hurry away and turned to Tony. "What does the note say?"

She steeled herself for his answer. He'd already said it contained a threat. Judging from the anger on his face when he'd read it, the threat was serious.

He moved to stand beside her and held the note where she could see it.

Large block print filled the page, written with a Sharpie.

YOUR TURN. I'M READY FOR BOTH YOUR DOG AND YOUR BOYFRIEND.

She looked up at Tony. "I'm leaving in less than twelve hours. If you can keep me safe that long and see me on my way, by this time tomorrow, I'll be arriving in Cincinnati."

"I'm not letting you out of my sight. Let's hurry and get what you need from your place." He looked at the other man. "You're following us?"

"All the way to the charter office, then others will take over."

As he walked away, Tony opened the back door of the Nissan. Bella hopped in and stretched out beside Gavin's car seat. "I know John will be sitting right out front, but I want to make this as quick as we can."

"Will do." If she forgot anything, she'd buy it in Ohio.

She climbed into the passenger seat and looked back at Bella. "You worked hard today. Good girl."

Her tail pounded the seat.

Tony cranked the engine and drove toward the park entrance. As he drew to a stop, waiting for traffic to clear, she looked in the side mirror. A dark Ford Explorer sat directly behind them, John at the wheel.

Tony pulled out, and she looked over at him. "I was really hoping you guys were going to catch this guy today. I know it was a long shot, but still."

"I had hoped so, too." He slid her a sideways glance before returning his eyes to the road. "I don't want you to leave."

She studied him, waiting for him to continue. He wasn't relaxed. She could see it in the tightness of his jaw, the tension in his shoulders, the way he was gripping the wheel. Was he developing feelings for her that went beyond friendship and wasn't sure how to tell her?

What about her own feelings? In spite of how hard she'd fought it, she was falling for him. A wave of guilt swept through her. If she was thinking of moving on this quickly, what did that say of the importance of what she'd had with Mark?

Seconds ticked by in silence, except for the hum of the Nissan's engine. If Tony was having romantic thoughts toward her, he didn't seem very anxious to admit it.

She released a sigh. "I don't *want* to leave."

Maybe she should make it easier for him and share her own feelings. But what if she was misreading him? What if he still thought of her as simply a close friend and she confessed to feeling more?

No, she'd been there, done that and was still embarrassed by it. If he wanted to pursue a romantic relationship with her, he was going to have to spell it out clearly… in neon. She wasn't about to put herself out there a second time.

She shifted her gaze to stare out the front windshield. "One good thing came out of today. Now you know you're not just looking for a pickup."

"I know. Either he ditched the pickup, or he owns more than one vehicle."

A heavy silence descended between them again, the weight of words not shared. He'd told her this morning about what had happened with his niece. Maybe he had let that be a barrier between them—the fear that something like that could happen again. They could work through that.

There was one other barrier, one that she didn't want to think about. Through her adolescence, her mother had often warned of the dangers of being "unequally yoked." Though she'd never said an unkind word about their father, Kris had been able to read between the lines: if she'd have married a man who shared her faith—not just shared it, but really tried to live it out—the relationships in their home would have been far different.

Tony would have been raised with the same strong beliefs. He'd apparently never wavered in his commitment to God. She and Kassie both had, but Kassie had come back. Kris would, too, when she was ready.

That day was getting closer. All of her excuses for walking away were crumbling. Her mother hadn't left her faith and her children. The results wouldn't be back for some time, but Kris didn't need positive identification to know that those bones hidden under the gazebo belonged to her mom. The Sanderson family hadn't failed her, either. Contrary to her father's lies, Jerry Sanderson had done nothing but show Christian love and kindness.

The only thing she still had to come to terms with was God taking Mark. Over the past eighteen months, she'd asked why dozens of times. She hadn't gotten an answer, or even any sign that God was listening. Maybe He was, and she just couldn't hear Him through the anger and mental and emotional anguish.

She let her head fall back against the seat, and soon her eyelids grew heavy. Tomorrow she'd have to be up before daylight, and she was already exhausted. The eleven-hour drive was going to require cold AC, upbeat music and multiple cups of coffee.

By the time they'd picked up Gavin from Ms. MaryAnn's it was dusk. Tony pulled into her driveway, and John parked the Explorer at the edge of the street.

When she reached for her door handle,

Tony held up his hand. "Wait here while I check the house."

"Good idea." She and Gavin and Bella would be safe with John sitting twenty feet away.

She handed him her keys, and he returned a few minutes later. "All clear. Let's make this fast."

As Tony headed to the living room with Bella, she removed a flashlight from the hall closet. The final remnants of afternoon sunlight drifting through the windows left most of the house in shadow. That minimal light wouldn't last long.

She picked up Gavin and hurried up the stairs. After putting him in his crib with a variety of toys, she clicked on the flashlight and entered the large walk-in closet. One large and one medium-size suitcase should do it. She laid them open on the bed. There was no time for her usual detailed packing list. She'd do her best, but she'd probably be making an emergency shopping trip in the near future.

She pulled a few pairs of jeans and dress

pants from the closet, then chose coordinating blouses. Next would be shorts and shirts. Shoes, too. All she'd brought to the charter office was her hiking boots, tennis shoes and a pair of boat shoes. She piled each item on the bed as it came to mind. What if her stay extended into late September or October, even November? She and Gavin would need warm clothes. Sweaters, jackets, mittens, knit hats. She heaved a sigh, suddenly stalled out.

The problem was she didn't want to make this trip. Under normal circumstances, she loved visiting her in-laws. She'd felt close to them almost immediately upon meeting them. But this was different. She was having to leave Tony, with no idea of when she'd see him again. Another pang of guilt stabbed her. Mark had been gone a year and a half. How long was long enough?

"Kris?" Tony's voice drifted up from the bottom of the stairs.

"Don't rush me." She snapped her mouth

closed, but the snippy words had already escaped. "I'm sorry. I'm almost done."

"I was just letting you know I'm taking Bella out. I think she needs to go. She's standing at attention at the front door."

"Go ahead. We'll be down in about ten minutes."

When she'd folded and packed her clothes into the larger suitcase, she started on Gavin's. Less than ten minutes later, she was ready.

"Come on, sweetie." She lifted him from the crib.

After wheeling both suitcases down the hall, she hollered at Tony from the top of the stairs. "We're done. Can you lug the suitcases down?"

No answer.

"Tony?"

He apparently hadn't come back inside yet. Ten minutes was more than enough time for Bella to do her business. Maybe he was at the road talking with John.

"Okay, buddy. Let's go find Mr. Tony. Hold Mommy's flashlight."

"'Kay."

Leaving the suitcases there, she picked up Gavin and headed down the stairs, the beam of the flashlight bouncing along the wall at her side. The light that had shone through the windows when she arrived was gone.

When she crossed the foyer to the front door, it was locked. That made sense. Tony wouldn't leave them in an unlocked house, even when he'd be right outside. Maybe he'd left her keys inside and was currently locked out.

After putting Gavin down, she swung the door open and stepped onto the porch. "Tony?"

Still no answer. Where was he? Had he walked Bella around back?

She glanced at the Explorer still sitting beside the road. She couldn't see inside. "Tony?"

Still no answer. The hair on the back of her neck stood on end. Something wasn't right.

She backed into the house. Before she

could get the door closed, a figure shot across the yard and charged up the front steps. She slammed the door. As she reached for the lock, the door exploded against her, knocking her into the Bombay chest on the opposite wall.

She screamed loud and long. Gavin stood a few feet away, clutching the flashlight, his own wail dissolving into hysterical sobs. An icy block of dread filled her chest. The boater stood staring down at her, holding an object she didn't recognize in his right hand, illuminated by the beam of the flashlight.

She stepped in front of Gavin, shielding him with her own body. He dropped the light and wrapped both arms around one of her legs, still sobbing.

"What do you want?" It was a stupid question, but maybe if she stalled, it would give Tony or John time to come to her aid.

"You're what I want." He looked down at Gavin. "This one's just insurance, something to guarantee that you'll cooperate."

He raised his arm. "Do you know what this is?"

The flashlight was still on, its beam making a diagonal path across the hardwood floor. It no longer illuminated what he held.

"It's a Taser. Have you ever seen what one of these can do to a full-grown man, especially when set on high? Right now, your boyfriend is lying in your side yard pretty much incapacitated. So is that plainclothes cop you had watching you. They'll both recover pretty quick. I'm not sure about the dog."

The panic over Bella's fate barely registered before the man pointed the weapon toward Gavin. "Just think what this could do to a little boy."

She dropped to her knees. "Please. Do whatever you want to me, but don't hurt my little boy."

"Take his hand. We're gonna walk outside to that white Nissan, and you're gonna drive us."

"I don't have the keys."

He reached into his front pocket with his free hand. When he pulled it out, a ring of keys dangled from his index finger.

Tony's keys.

He'd been in such bad shape the killer had been able to take his keys without him putting up a fight. How could one man sneak up on two trained police officers and incapacitate them both?

As her abductor led her to the vehicle sitting in the drive, he held the Taser flat against his chest, inconspicuous to anyone who might happen to see them. But there was no one outside, no kids riding bicycles, no adults on evening strolls.

He opened the driver door and the one behind it, then reached for Gavin's hand. The little boy drew back, clinging to her leg, cries renewed.

"Tell him to get in the back."

"I'll put him in his car seat. Come here, sweetie."

She lifted him into the vehicle. After he'd climbed into his seat, she struggled to clip the straps with shaking hands.

"Don't bother fastening him in. He won't be there long."

She swiveled her head to look over her shoulder, fear almost immobilizing her. "What are you going to do to him?"

"Nothing if you follow my instructions exactly."

He grabbed her by the hair to pull her from the vehicle. After shoving her into the front seat, he climbed in behind her. "Drive."

He directed her around a couple of corners. "Pull over here."

She did as instructed and shifted the vehicle into Park. They'd hardly left her neighborhood. Two houses stood across the street, a small patch of trees to her immediate right.

"Get out."

"What about Gavin?"

"Get him out, too."

After scrambling from the vehicle, she leaned into the back to pull her son from his car seat. He had stopped crying some time ago, but his body shook with each shuddering breath. She clutched him to her chest and glanced around her. The front end of a car was barely visible between two of the trees.

The man gripped her upper arm and led her to an old Oldsmobile, its body a dingy gray in the moonlight that filtered through the trees. Likely the same car Noah had described.

After taking Tony's keys from her, he tossed them some distance away and handed her a different set. "Put your kid in the back and get in."

She did what he'd told her. There was no car seat, but that was the least of her concerns. Soon they were again on their way, eventually headed west on 98. A couple of miles from the Florida–Alabama line, he instructed her to take a left. Where was he taking them?

Shortly after she'd reached the 55-mile-an-hour speed limit, he tapped her on the shoulder. "Pull over here."

She pressed the brakes and came to a stop on the shoulder, in front of a brown

Tarkiln Bayou Preserve State Park sign. There were no other vehicles, and both the entry and exit gates were closed and locked.

"Hand me the keys."

She turned off the car and passed the keys to him. When she looked back at her little boy, his thumb was in his mouth, and his eyes were round in the light of a half-moon. Her heart squeezed in a painful combination of love and fear.

God, if you're listening, please protect my boy. I don't deserve any favors, but little Gavin is so young and innocent.

"Get out of the car."

The terse command cut across her thoughts, and she scrambled onto the asphalt shoulder. The road wasn't well traveled. No one had come from either direction during the minute or so they'd been stopped.

The killer climbed from the back seat, pulling Gavin out with him. "Come on, little boy. We're going for a walk."

Kris's thoughts spun. What was he going

to do to them? Did he plan to take them into the woods and kill them? The park covered more than four thousand acres. How long would it be before someone discovered their bodies? Was he going to do to them what he did to the woman she and Tony discovered? A shudder shook her shoulders and rippled down her spine.

He moved into the woods, Gavin's hand in one of his, the Taser in the other. She had no choice but to follow. After traveling about forty feet, he released her little boy's hand and turned to face her. "We're going back to the car now."

What? Did he change his mind? What was the point of their little detour?

She picked up her son, and he wrapped both arms around her neck. She'd hardly gone two steps when the man's words stopped her cold.

"Not him. You and me."

She spun and squeezed Gavin so hard he squirmed in her grasp. "We can't leave him alone out here in the dark."

"Actually, we can and we will. The question is whether we leave him conscious or unconscious. Dead or alive. Put him down."

"No, I can't…" Her throat closed up, and her brain stalled out. The killer was letting Gavin go, but he was leaving him alone in a deserted park, pine trees all around, water just past the end of a long catwalk.

Warning flared in the man's eyes, and he held up the Taser.

"Please, let me take him somewhere safe."

The warning turned to anger. He flipped a switch and the red light of a laser appeared.

"This is armed, ready to fire. As you can see, your son is the target. So let's try this again. Put him down."

She lowered Gavin to the ground, and he held up both hands, sobbing. When he called for her, her heart broke. The killer gave her arm a yank, and she bit back a shriek.

"You might want to make sure he stays here so he doesn't get run over."

"Please let me talk to him."

Although he didn't give her permission, his hold on her relaxed.

She dropped to her knees again and hugged Gavin to her chest. "Baby, you stay right here. Put your arms around this tree and don't move until a nice policeman comes for you. Can you do that?"

He nodded, his eyes round. Big tears made rivulets down both cheeks.

She guided his arms around a pine. "Hang on to this tree and don't let go." He was just obedient enough to do it, all night if that was how long it took.

The man pulled her to her feet and gave her a shove. She stumbled forward, then cast a glance over her shoulder. "Mommy loves you so much, but she has to go with this man." She choked back a sob.

He dragged her toward the car, and cries of "Mommy" followed them, shredding her heart even further. A sense of hopelessness descended on her, and the tears she'd managed to hold at bay for her son's sake flowed freely.

God, whatever happens to me, please protect my little boy.

When they reached the car, instead of directing her to the driver's side, he kept a tight grip on her arm while he opened the trunk.

"Get in."

She shook her head, trying to back away. "Please don't put me in the trunk."

He glanced toward the woods, fingering the Taser. He didn't say a thing. He didn't have to. The silent threat was just as effective as any words he might use. She scrambled into the trunk and sat, hip wedged against the spare tire.

"Good girl. I think I'll even reward you by making a little phone call." He touched three numbers and pressed the phone to his ear. "I'm calling to report a child left unattended at Tarkiln Bayou State Park. A little boy, about two or three."

Without waiting for a response, he ended the call. Kris slumped forward, face against her knees and shoulders shaking with sobs she didn't even try to hold back. But now her tears were those of relief.

"Thank you." She lifted her head and drew in a shuddering breath. "Thank you, thank you."

And thank you, God. He'd answered her prayer.

Her abductor's lips curled back in a sneer. "I did it for him, not you. He doesn't deserve to suffer. You do."

Without any warning, his fist slammed into the side of her head. Stars exploded across her vision, tiny points of light that rapidly faded and disappeared. Darkness encroached from all sides, slowly extinguishing the moon's soft glow.

The trunk's lid slammed closed.

The suffering he mentioned had begun.

NINE

Tony struggled to his hands and knees, muscles still in spasm from a sustained Taser shock. One minute, he'd been following Bella around the side of the house, waiting for her to do her business. The next he'd had 50,000 volts of electricity coursing through his body with nothing more than the one-second warning of a twig snapping behind him.

He'd just started to recover from the Taser shock when his attacker had pressed a stun gun to his neck, and the excruciating pain had begun anew.

He'd heard Kris step outside and call his name but hadn't been able to respond. His jaw had been clenched, and every muscle in his body had contracted and released in rapid, painful spasms. Then he'd lost consciousness.

He pushed himself fully upright and pulled one barb from his abdomen and the other from his hip. Bella was lying a few feet away, whimpering. When the man had attacked him, the dog had approached growling, her stance aggressive. Without letting his finger off the Taser's trigger, he'd jammed the stun gun against the dog's neck then finished him off.

"Hang on, girl." He'd have to see to the dog later. He stumbled toward the front of the house on sluggish legs, reaching for his radio with one hand, his weapon with the other.

His weapon was gone.

He radioed dispatch to request backup. His attacker could still be on the property, possibly even inside with Kris and Gavin.

He crept forward. As he rounded the front corner of the house, his gaze swept the driveway, and his stomach dropped. The Nissan was gone.

He charged up the porch steps, willing

his stubborn limbs to hurry. The front door was open, a flashlight's beam shining across the foyer floor.

"Kris?" He stopped at the bottom of the stairs and hollered again, knowing all along that the darkened house was empty.

He could guess what had happened while he was out. The man who'd attacked him had gone after Kris and taken both her and Gavin away in the Nissan. A vise clamped down on his chest, and his knees went suddenly weak. *Oh, God, please keep them both safe.*

He radioed dispatch again with an update. "We have a kidnapping. We're looking for a white 2023 Nissan Rogue."

Or maybe not. The man had probably parked his own vehicle nearby and traded them out. "Also put out an APB for a white Chevy pickup, maybe around 1995. An older gray sedan, too."

He stepped back onto the porch. Where was John? How could this happen with two trained police officers protecting her?

He approached the Explorer and opened

the driver door. Light flooded the interior. John was gone.

Using the flashlight on his phone, he circled the house. When he reached the back, he swept the beam of light around the yard. Jean-covered legs and shoes were barely visible at the edge of a small grouping of trees. He hurried in that direction, his heart in his throat.

When the legs drew up, Tony released a relieved breath. He might be injured, but he was at least alive.

He dropped to his knees next to his fellow law enforcement officer. Rope secured his ankles. His arms wrapped the tree trunk behind him, his wrists bound on the other side. A piece of duct tape covered his mouth. Two wires trailed away from him, the probes apparently behind him.

"This is going to hurt." Tony reached for the tape and gave it a swift yank. "What happened?"

John barely winced. "I thought I might have seen movement next to the house but wasn't sure."

While he continued his explanation, Tony untied his hands.

"I drew my weapon, went to investigate. Next thing I knew, I was getting Tased from behind. Didn't think the creep was ever going to let off the trigger. By the time I could move again, he had me bound and gagged."

When his hands were free, he rubbed one wrist and then the other before reaching down to release his ankles. "What about the lady and her boy? I heard a vehicle start up and feared the worst."

Tony pressed his lips together, the tightness in his chest returning full force. "You're right. They're gone. Do you have your weapon?"

"No. The guy took it as soon as he had me tied up." He pushed himself to his feet. "You want to pull those things out of my back? I'm not sure I can reach them."

Tony moved behind him. One probe had hit the center of his left shoulder blade and the other a couple of inches below his waist.

He removed them one at a time. "I hate to admit it, but I'm in the same boat you are—surprised, Tased and disarmed."

Sirens sounded in the distance, and John glanced in that direction. "I'm guessing you already called it in."

"Yep. I'm going to check on the dog. She got zapped with a stun gun."

John headed toward the front, while Tony continued across the back of the house to the other side. Bella had risen and was plodding away from him on unsteady legs.

"Bella."

The dog turned to look at him and released another whimper. He hurried toward her and took her face in his hands. Then he massaged her, from her neck all the way down her back. "Are you all right?"

She pressed her face against his leg and wagged her tail.

When they reached the driveway, two Pensacola Police cruisers drew to a stop at the edge of Kris's front yard, lights flashing. Lettering on one identified it as a K-9 unit.

The driver door swung open, and Jared Miles stepped out, creases of concern etched into his features. "It's Kris, isn't it?"

He nodded. "Gavin, too. The guy came out of nowhere, Tased me."

He'd promised to keep them safe. How could he have let this happen?

Jared put a hand on his shoulder. "You did what you could."

He swallowed hard. "Can you let Kassie know?"

She'd pray until Kris was found, adding strength to his own incessant, desperate prayers.

"Sure." He stepped to the side and pulled his phone from his pocket. While he made the call, the other officer approached.

"Rick Danforth. Can you fill us in on what happened?"

As Danforth jotted down a few notes, their radios crackled to life. The authorities had found the Nissan. Tony had guessed right. It wasn't much more than a block away. That meant Kris and Gavin were likely in either the white pickup or the gray sedan.

The dispatcher's voice came through their radios a second time, dispatching units to Tarkiln Bayou Preserve State Park. They'd received an anonymous call about an abandoned child.

Tony looked at John. The rental car would be out of commission until Crime Scene finished processing it. "Can you take me there? Depending on the circumstances, we might need Bella."

"Absolutely." John headed toward the Explorer, digging his keys from his pocket.

Tony whistled for the dog and fell in next to him. "It's got to be Gavin. Someone discovering a lost child would stay with him until the police arrived. The call was anonymous. This person doesn't want to be discovered, but he also didn't want harm to come to the boy."

"Why take him and leave him in the park? Why not leave him here?"

"What better way to ensure Kris's cooperation than to threaten her son?"

"Makes sense. The timing is right, too. Almost twenty minutes has passed since I heard your car start up. Tarkiln Bayou Park is about ten minutes southwest of here. That leaves enough time for him to switch vehicles, drive to the park, drop off the boy and make the call."

John climbed into the driver's seat, and Tony circled around to the passenger side to let Bella into the back. Before getting in, he hollered at the men still standing in the drive.

"Have them search the area for the Chevy pickup and gray sedan I called in earlier. Check along 98, going west." It wouldn't make sense for the killer to go to the park and then head east on 98, backtracking through Pensacola. No, they were heading west, into Alabama.

God, please let the authorities catch up with them before they leave the highway.

Tony slid in opposite John and sent up yet another prayer of protection for both Kris and Gavin. When John stopped in front of the closed entry gate ten minutes later, two marked units had just arrived. He and John stepped over the gate and into the parking lot with the four officers.

Tony took charge. "Let's spread out." He pointed to one of the men. "You, follow the catwalk and check the water's edge." He motioned to two others. "One of you take the woods to the right of the catwalk, the other the woods to the left. The rest of us will fan out from there. We think the little boy's name is Gavin."

Bella suddenly stood at attention, staring into the woods, body rigid with tension.

"What is it, girl? Do you hear something?"

The dog barked once, and a ripple went through her body.

He looked at the men "Go. Start your search. We'll keep in touch via radio."

Without waiting for a response, he bent over to hold Bella's face in his hands. "You know where he is, don't you, girl?" He straightened and held out a hand, index finger extended. "Go find Gavin."

Bella trotted into the woods, sniffing the air the same way she'd done when they'd searched for the missing camper. After going a few yards, she came to a sudden stop, her ears lifting slightly.

The next moment, she charged ahead, leaving Tony scrambling to keep up. Soon he lost sight of her.

"Bella. Where are you, girl?"

After several moments of silence, excited barks echoed through the woods. He ran toward the sound. The dog was sitting on her haunches in the patchy moonlight, Gavin in front of her.

He sat on the ground, legs extended in front of him, arms wrapped around a tree to his right. Now that Bella had fallen silent, Tony could pick up what the dog had apparently heard—soft whimpers.

Tony spoke into his radio. "The child is found."

He dropped to his knees next to the little

boy. Although the dog was pressed against him, he still sat with his arms wrapped around the tree.

"Come here, buddy. Let Uncle Tony take you home."

Gavin let go of the rough trunk and reached out his hands. Tony picked him up and held him against his chest, whatever uneasiness he'd once had completely gone. Little arms went around his neck, and warmth filled his chest. Thanks to Bella, he'd found Kris's little boy and played a part in his rescue.

Without relaxing his embrace on Gavin, he rose and headed back toward the front gate. God had answered his prayer. Half of it, anyway. He lifted his eyes heavenward, gratitude swelling inside.

Thank you, God, for keeping Gavin safe. Please do the same for Kris.

Pain. The full length of her body. It was everywhere—her ankles, her hip, her wrists, her shoulder, her head…

Especially her head.

Where was all the pain coming from? She struggled to open her eyes, but her eyelids seemed to be weighted down.

After a couple more attempts, they slid open a sliver. Scuffed hardwood planks extended some distance in front of her, running under a small table and disappearing at a log wall. She was on the floor of what looked like a rundown cabin. A man sat at the table nursing a can of soda or beer, a lantern burning in front of him.

Kris let her eyes fall shut again. Where was she?

When she tried to shift her position, she couldn't do it. Her hands were tied behind her back, her ankles bound. Tape covered her mouth.

Memory rushed back to her with the force of a tidal wave. The boater had abducted her. He'd somehow gotten past both Tony and John. He'd taken her son, too.

But Gavin was safe. The man had called the police. By now, her boy would be in Mildred's care, or possibly Kassie's.

She tried to lift her head, and a moan escaped through her nose. The figure in the chair shifted. The next moment, a blinding light shone in her face, and she squeezed her eyes shut again.

"After two hours, you finally decided to join the party. I guess I hit you harder than I intended. Sometimes I don't know my own strength."

She opened one eye a sliver. Nothing existed except that blinding beam of light, which cast everything else into total blackness.

Suddenly, it clicked off, and his chair scraped against the hardwood floor. She watched him rise and approach, his footsteps slow and deliberate.

He stopped in front of her and knelt down. "I'm going to pull the tape now. Don't bother to scream, because there aren't any people for miles. You'll just tick me off, which would be a huge mistake."

He picked at one corner of the tape until he had enough loose to get a good grip. Then he ripped it away in one angry motion. Fire shot through the lower part of her face. She winced but didn't cry out. Based on the condition of the victim she and Tony had found in the woods, losing a few skin cells was probably pleasant compared to what he had in store for her.

He stood and pulled an object from his pocket. It didn't look like the Taser, but with the lantern at his back, she couldn't say for sure.

For several moments, he stared down at her, his face cast in shadow. Was he trying to decide what to do with her? Or was the wait part of the torment?

He flicked his wrist and a blade extended. Panic pounded up her spine. He was going to stab her to death like he did Shannon.

Instead, he stepped over her. For a good half minute, she held her breath, waiting for the piercing pain of a knife wound or a boot to the kidney or another blow to the head.

It didn't come. One large hand wrapped hers, and the smooth edges of the knife slid between her wrists. With a couple of rapid, upward slices, she was free.

She pushed herself into a seated position, her legs extended in front of her. Soon he had sawed through the bindings securing her ankles. He lifted her to her feet and threw her into the other kitchen chair.

Over the next several minutes, he finished his beer and pulled another one from a cooler against the wall. The place likely didn't have electricity, even if the power had been restored. If he wanted cool beverages, he'd have to make it to a store sometime in the next few days. Or maybe he planned to kill her before his ice ran out.

He sat across from her again and popped the top on his beer. "Are you thirsty?"

She looked at him with raised brows. Was he showing a smidgeon of concern? She'd pass on the beer, but a bottle of cold water was really appealing. "A little."

"Good."

He took a long swig of the beer. As the

minutes ticked by, he made no move to get her anything. Instead, he picked up a small block of wood and shaved slivers off of it with the knife he'd used to cut her bindings.

She looked around the cabin. It was small, the main part a single room that housed a small living area and a kitchen-ette. At the end of the short counter, an open door led into a darkened room, prob-ably a bedroom.

Where were they? Were they still in Florida, or had he taken her to Georgia or Alabama? He said she'd been out for two hours. That meant they could even be in Mississippi.

Looking outside didn't offer any clue as to her whereabouts. All was dark beyond the four cracked and dirt-caked windows. Come morning, she might be able to see through them.

When she met his eyes again, he was watching her. "You're probably won-dering where we are. We're deep in the woods where no one will find us. This place has sat undisturbed since before I was a teenager."

He returned to his carving, his movements rhythmic. Outside, the high-pitched buzz of cicadas formed a muffled backdrop for the scrape of his knife against the wood.

"You know, you're special. Not like the others. I've got you, but you made me work for it. Trust me, you'll pay for those times you thwarted my plans."

He spoke without looking at her, his attention on the block of wood in his hand. He cut off another thin slice, letting it fall to the growing pile of shavings already there. If what remained of the original block was supposed to be a work of art, it hadn't begun to take shape yet.

"You were actually doing me a favor, because it'll be so much more satisfying in the end. A prize worked for is more rewarding than one that comes too easily."

He laid down the wood and then folded the knife. Leaving the beer can sitting on the table, he walked to the cooler again and returned with a bottle of water. Without a word, he plunked it on the small table, sat and resumed sipping his beer.

Kris eyed the water bottle, droplets of moisture clinging to it. It was sitting between them, closer to her than it was to him. Had he intended it for her?

She could surely use it. While searching for survivors in the park, she'd tried to stay well hydrated. That was hard to do in the sun with temperatures in the mid-nineties. She hadn't had anything to drink since arriving at home, and she was beyond thirsty.

She looked at him for silent permission, but he had resumed his carving.

"Thank you for the water." If he didn't want her to have it, he'd stop her.

Except for the jerky movements of the knife, he was still, his eyes fixed on his project.

She slowly reached for the bottle, giving him plenty of opportunity to intervene. She clasped her hand around it, slid it closer, unscrewed the lid.

She touched the top to her lips, and cool, refreshing water flowed into her mouth. His chair scraped across the hardwood floor. Before she could react, his open hand connected with her cheek, sending the bottle flying. It landed on its side against the wall, water pouring from its top.

She pressed a hand to her stinging cheek. He'd set her up.

"These games aren't so much fun, are they? It's a lot different being on the receiving end."

What games? Before she had a chance to voice her question aloud, he jerked her up from the chair, one meaty hand wrapped around her upper arm. Her shoulder gave a crack of protest.

"Now it's your turn to be hungry and thirsty." He dragged her toward the doorway into the darkened room, and she stumbled after him. The space had probably been a bedroom at one time, but the only sign of its former use was a dilapidated chest of drawers standing in one corner, a two-foot-by-three-foot window nearby.

He stopped in front of a closed door, likely a closet, still maintaining his vise-like grip on her arm. "I hated the dark, but you didn't care."

She looked at him in the soft glow of the lantern spilling in from the main room. What was he talking about?

After swinging open the door, he threw her inside, slamming her body into the back wall. "Now you're going to pay."

The door banged shut, leaving her in pitch blackness except for the sliver of dim light that found its way under the door. "It's finally your turn to be locked in a dark closet."

Instead of leaving the room, he paced for some time outside the closet door. "Are you sorry yet?"

Sorry for what? Evading him?

As he paced the room, she felt the walls for any weak boards that might offer a means of escape. There were none.

If he left her alone and she could escape

the closet, maybe she could climb through the bedroom window. She reached for the doorknob and turned it slowly. It moved about one-eighth of a turn and stopped. It was locked.

He suddenly banged on the door, and she drew back her hand with a stifled shriek.

"How does it feel, Lana?"

Footsteps retreated, and another door slammed.

"I'm not Lana." Her shouted denial probably didn't even reach him.

A sense of hopelessness bore down on her, threatening to crush her. She was trapped in a remote cabin with a madman with little chance of rescue.

She sank down the wall and sat on the floor, knees drawn up to her chest. The small space didn't allow for any other position.

She wasn't Lana, had never met her and had no idea who she was.

But she was paying for every one of her sins.

TEN

Tony walked from the police department building, shoulders slouched and worry gnawing a hole in his gut. They'd soon be coming up on twenty-four hours since Kris was taken and were nowhere near finding her. He'd put in a long shift, tracking down every lead they'd gotten. There hadn't been many. At different times throughout the day and early evening, all the local television stations had been airing the composite Kris had done a couple of weeks ago.

With tens of thousands of homes without power, it wasn't having near the impact it normally would. The only people with the ability to view what was being aired were those with backup generators or battery-operated, digital-ready TVs with exterior antennas.

Even so, the police had gotten two leads. One was from an older man, calling about a guy who had moved in next door to him a couple of weeks ago. Tony had to admit there was a resemblance, but it wasn't a strong one. After talking to the guy, his employer and his family, they'd eliminated him. The other lead had been an even bigger stretch.

Several agencies had put helicopters in the air, looking for either vehicle, as well as anything that might provide clues in the case.

Tony tried to not think about what she was experiencing—the fear, the terror, the emotional and physical suffering. The killer had intended to silence her the way he'd silenced Shannon. How long had it taken him to realize Kris fit the profile of his victims? Not long, based on the pictures found in the motel room. Sometime between her encountering him when he'd dumped the camper's body and the night of the storm, she had moved from a witness to be silenced to another victim to torment. He'd made that clear in his phone call.

Tony slid into the driver's seat of his department-assigned vehicle. If he had any idea where Kris's abductor had taken her, he'd get out there and search for her himself.

One thing was sure. The man hadn't followed Highway 98, at least not for any length of time. Several agencies had swarmed the highway for miles in both directions, searching for the white Chevy truck and the gray sedan. Either Kris's abductor had fled in yet another vehicle, or he'd traveled some distance away from 98.

Last night, he and John had dropped Gavin off with Kassie, then retrieved his department-assigned vehicle. He'd also left Bella there, with the understanding that he'd be picking her up again if there was any chance she could assist in finding Kris. Unfortunately, he had no idea where to even begin looking.

He cranked the vehicle and shifted into reverse. Processing the Nissan had turned up nothing. The prints they'd identified were his. The ones not in the system had probably belonged to Kris.

They were all out of options. Except prayer. Of course, he'd been praying almost nonstop since Kris disappeared. So had Kassie and Jared and his mom and dad. Nick and Joanne, too.

Last night, he'd almost told her how he felt. He'd said he didn't want her to leave. He'd meant it with every fiber of his being. She'd waited for him to continue. He hadn't been able to bring himself to do it. He wasn't the father her little boy should have. He'd never be able to step into the shoes of the man smiling out from the frame on her fireplace mantle. So what was the point of telling her that he was falling for her when they'd never be more than friends?

But maybe he should have, because now he was looking at the possibility of losing her, leaving all those words forever unsaid. *God, please let me see her again.*

He'd almost reached the edge of the parking lot when his cell phone rang. When he looked at the screen, his pulse kicked into high gear. His captain was calling him.

"Hey, Keith."

"You'd better get back in here."

Tony pulled into the nearest parking space, heart pounding. "What's going on?"

"There's a guy here you'll want to talk to."

After killing the engine, he jumped from the vehicle and jogged toward the building. Light poured out from inside, the backup generators having kicked in right after the power went out two nights ago. When he reached his captain's office, another detective, Robbie Sanchez, was standing there, along with a man Tony had never met.

Keith stood and made introductions, then continued. "Kenny here is pretty sure he knows our guy."

Kenny nodded. "I grew up in Perdido,

Alabama, about an hour northwest of here. Moved to Pensacola about five years ago. From age thirteen on, there was another kid I used to hang with, Brent Wadsworth. Although I haven't seen him for about two years now, the composite I saw on TV looks just like him."

"How about a last known address?"

"Last time I talked to him, he was living in Cantonment, about a half hour north of here."

"Did he mention where?" Sanchez asked. "A street name or anything?"

"No."

Tony frowned. "After taking the lady from her home on Bayou Texar, we know he stopped by Tarkiln Bayou Preserve State Park. If he was headed toward Cantonment, that detour would have taken him far out of his way."

Kenny nodded. "That park is just a little way off 98, right?"

"It is."

"If he hopped back on 98 and headed west into Alabama, after ten or fifteen minutes, he could drive north for an hour and run right into Perdido, our old stomping grounds."

"Is there somewhere around there that you think he might have taken her?"

Kenny pursed his lips, brows drawn together in concentration. "It's a long shot. I don't know if I could even find it. When we were fifteen, Brent discovered an old, abandoned cabin in the woods. We used to hike to it and hang out."

Tony looked at Keith. "I'd like to pick up Bella and have Kenny try to take us out there."

"Go. Meet back here in thirty minutes. We'll have a group ready to go."

Tony hurried from the building, dialing Kassie as he walked. She answered on the second ring.

"I'm picking up Bella. We have a lead."

He didn't want to get her hopes up in case it didn't pan out. But she probably needed a spark of hope as badly as he did.

"That's awesome. I'll be praying even harder, if that's possible."

When he arrived at Kassie's a few minutes later, she was waiting out front for him, Bella in her vest, her leash attached to her collar.

She handed him the looped end. "Text me as soon as you know something."

"I will."

He opened the back door for the dog. "How is Gavin handling everything?"

"Not well. He keeps crying for his mother."

Tony's heart twisted. The poor child lost his father. *God, please don't take his mother away, too.*

When he returned to the station, plans were well underway. Besides Sanchez, Jared Miles was there with his dog, Justice.

Keith walked them all outside. "We're coordinating with a SWAT team out of Mobile. Everyone will rendezvous in the Perdido Elementary School parking lot."

Tony looked at his captain. "I'd like to have Kenny ride with me if that's okay."

Keith nodded. "Sure."

"We'll be the lead vehicle, since Kenny is the only one who knows where we're going."

"I'll do my best, anyway."

Tony hurried to his vehicle, Kenny following. When they'd both climbed into their seats, he pulled from the parking lot and made his way toward 98, struggling to keep his speed down to a justifiable level.

Kenny looked over at him. "I understand this lady isn't the only one."

"She's not."

"I've been on vacation up in Wisconsin for the past two weeks, so I didn't see the composite aired until tonight."

"That's understandable."

"These women and the one you're looking for, are they dark-haired, slender build, fairly attractive?"

Tony cast him a sideways glance. "Yeah. Why do you ask?"

"His sister was dark-haired."

Several moments passed in silence. Tony eased to a stop at a darkened traffic light. When he looked at the other man, he was frowning. "Did he not get along with his sister?"

"It was a lot worse than that." Kenny's face was creased in the soft moonlight. "Their mother left them alone a lot, usually left his older sister in charge of him. She apparently resented being responsible for her kid brother and took it out on him."

After checking for traffic both directions, Tony pressed the gas. "She hit him?"

"Yeah. Tormented him other ways, too."

"Do you know where she is, his sister?"

"No. I never met her. They were both removed from the home when he was six and she was thirteen, then adopted into different families. But he had a couple of pictures of her."

Several more seconds passed in silence. There was more to the story, something that apparently bothered Kenny all these years later.

"Tell me about these pictures."

"They looked like school pictures. He showed them to me a couple of times." He sucked in a deep breath. "Brent used to draw a lot, make pencil sketches of animals, superheroes, people he knew, you name it. He had a lot of talent. But the sketches he did of his sister were really disturbing."

"Disturbing in what way?"

"In a lot of the drawings, she was bound and gagged. In all of them, she'd been beaten or shot or stabbed. They were really graphic for being done in charcoal pencil."

"Did he say the girl in the drawings was his sister?"

"Yeah. Even though it was obvious, I asked. He used to say that someday she was going to pay for the way she treated him. I always told him to let it go, that she wasn't worth the energy he was expending on her. I even talked to the school counselor once."

"How did that go?"

"She didn't let him know that I had said anything. She just brought him in and talked to him about his home life, both with his adoptive family and with his birth mother. Brent had been through counseling before and had figured out how to give all the right answers. He was good at acting totally chill, like nothing bothered him. The counselors never saw the side of him that I saw. He could go from happy to furious and back to happy again without breaking stride." Kenny sighed. "Now I find out I was friends with a possible future serial killer. I should have pushed harder."

"Hey, don't beat yourself up. You did a lot more than most teenagers would have done. You had no way of knowing this would happen. It wasn't your fault, so don't carry the guilt for it."

He turned right onto 98. They were now headed west, the Alabama border not too far ahead. In a little over an hour, they'd meet up with the Mobile SWAT team.

"How many has he killed so far?"

Kenny's voice held a lot of heaviness, the weight of regret. Tony hoped he'd figure out how to let it go.

"Four." If they didn't find Kris tonight, she'd likely be number five.

No, he wouldn't even go there.

The man sitting beside him was the best lead they'd had since Amanda Driscoll disappeared from Milligan almost four months earlier.

Would this lead be a dead end too?

God, please help us find them.

And please don't let it be too late.

Kris dragged her eyes open and lifted her head with a moan. She was back in the closet. Judging from the fact that there was no sliver of light under the door, it was night. She'd lost all track of time, each painful hour bleeding into the next.

The last thing she remembered was sitting, tied to the kitchen chair, while her captor delivered blows to her head, face and stomach. It wasn't the first beating she'd received that day, but it was the worst. She'd apparently lost consciousness.

She closed her eyes and let her head rest against her knees. From what she'd gathered listening to his disjointed stories, Lana was an older sister who had subjected him to a lot of abuse. How many of the stories were true and how many were the creation of a tormented imagination didn't matter. She was paying for every bit of that abuse, whether real or imagined.

The bedroom door creaked open, and the soft glow of the lantern shone under the closet door. Her breath caught in her throat. As his heavy footsteps moved closer, her heart pounded out an erratic rhythm. What punishment was he going to mete out this time?

The knob rattled, and the door swung open. She sat huddled on the floor, unable to rise. Not only did her entire body hurt, her ankles were bound and her hands were lashed together behind her back. He'd bound her hands in the early morning hours. After she'd kicked him in a futile attempt to avoid his fists, he'd bound her feet also.

He'd never reapplied the tape over her mouth. There hadn't been a need. Screaming would only make things worse. He'd warned her.

She didn't lift her head until the toe of his boot slammed into her side.

"Wake up. It's time."

Time? Time for another beating or time to die?

He gripped her upper arm and hauled her to her feet. Then he threw her roughly over his shoulder. As he walked into the multipurpose room, she lifted her head to scan the space. One chair was angled away from the table, a beer can sitting there. The lantern shone from its usual spot in the center of the table.

Next to it lay a hammer.

No, no, no. He was finally finished toying with her. It was time for her to join the others.

He crossed the room and stopped a few feet from the door. Instead of bending to put her on the floor, he flipped her over and dropped her from shoulder height. She landed on her back, face up, arms trapped beneath her. The blow forced a grunt from her mouth.

When she tried to draw in a breath, her lungs seized up. No matter how she tried, her chest and throat remained paralyzed. Her heart slammed against her ribcage, and her thoughts spun. The panic gripping her probably made it worse, but she couldn't keep it at bay.

Her captor walked to the table, gait relaxed. The invisible bonds around her chest began to release, and she struggled in a constricted breath. The breaths that followed became easier.

When he turned to face her again, he was holding the hammer. The panic began anew. She was going to die. In the span of less than two years, little Gavin would lose both his father and his mother. But Mark's parents would raise him. They were good people.

And Tony. She should have told him how she felt about him. Instead, she was getting ready to pass from this life with all those emotions unexpressed.

And what about God? She'd let the fire she'd had as a child die when she'd thought her mother had left. When Mark had been killed, she'd finished stamping out what little spark remained. Now she was going to meet a God she'd spent the last ten years ignoring.

The killer slowly circled her, tapping the head of the hammer against his other palm, his gaze predatory.

This was it. Any second now, he'd start swinging.

God, please forgive me. Prepare me to meet You. Please watch over Gavin. And please somehow let Tony know that I love him.

The man completed another circle then stopped in front of her. His jaw was tight, his eyes narrowed. "Aren't you going to say something?"

She stared at him in dumb silence. What was she supposed to say?

He gripped the head of the hammer with his other hand. "I hold all power over you.

I hold the power of life and the power of death."

He was right. And it only made her situation that much more hopeless. He needed to just do what he was going to do and get it over with.

Anger flared in his eyes. "Say something."

What? Was he actually wanting her to talk him out of it?

No. Nothing she could say would make him rethink what he was about to do. He wanted her to plead for her life.

Was that what Shannon had done? Probably. Each of the other women, too. And he'd gotten some perverted thrill from listening to their pleas, a heady sense of power, finally being the one in control.

She wouldn't give it to him.

She wouldn't beg for mercy, but she wasn't giving up, either.

"You're right. You do have all the power. You have the power to take my life, to leave my little boy an orphan. But you also have the power to make the right choice, to be better than Lana. She was cruel. No one deserved to be treated the way she treated you."

The anger left his eyes as suddenly as it had come. Instead, there was hesitation. Maybe she was getting through to him. Was it her sympathy with his plight that was reaching him, or was he able to relate, just a little bit, to Gavin? She'd continue to hit him with both.

"I'm sorry you had a cruel sister instead of a loving mother." Maybe she was going out on a limb, but a loving mother wouldn't have let anyone torment him so severely. "You're better than Lana. You can rise above all the wrong she did to you." She pushed herself to a seated position, hands still tied behind her. "You met my son. You saw what a sweet little boy he is. He might even remind you of yourself at that age."

He lowered the hammer slowly until both hands came to rest at his sides. Had she actually talked him out of killing her?

"Every little boy deserves to grow up

with a loving mother. You deserved that, and I'm so sorry you didn't get it. But please don't take that away from my little boy."

She waited for a response but didn't get one. Instead, he continued to stare down at her, lips pressed together, creases of indecision between his eyebrows. If he'd just say something, anything.

"Please untie me and let me go back to my son." Since she'd been unconscious when he'd brought her in, she had no idea where to go. But if she could get out of the cabin, she'd figure it out.

His eyes widened and his lips curled back in a sneer. "No!"

The single word was a bellow, so sharp and loud she flinched.

"I'll never let you go. You have to pay."

He raised the hammer and swung it downward in an arc. As she twisted and rolled, the hammer's head grazed her shoulder. Pain shot all the way down her arm.

When he swung a second time, she

rolled again, and the metal end missed her head by mere millimeters.

For the past twenty-four hours, she'd heeded his warning not to scream. Now she screamed. She couldn't help it. It didn't matter that it was pointless, that no one would hear her. After the first scream came another and another, rising up from somewhere inside, seemingly of their own accord. Fear, anger and hopelessness melded together, too violent to contain.

This was it. He had won. And it wouldn't end here. He'd continue to kill, again and again.

He raised the hammer again.

Resisting was only delaying the inevitable. But she wouldn't make it easy on him.

She wouldn't give up until she had no strength left to fight.

ELEVEN

Tony zigzagged between trees at a full jog, Bella next to him. Jared was on his other side, Justice just ahead of them. Counting Kenny, Robbie Sanchez and the four SWAT guys out of Mobile, there were currently eight men and two dogs crashing through the trees.

But there was no time for the stealth they'd all started with. The enraged bellow and the subsequent high-pitched screams had told them all that Kris's time was almost up.

God, let us get there before it's too late.

Another scream split the night. It set every nerve in his body on edge, but it also sent relief flooding him. As long as Kris was screaming, she was still alive.

They all charged into a small clearing. Just ahead, a dilapidated cabin sat washed in the unfiltered glow of a swollen half-moon. Without slowing, Tony slammed his shoulder into the door.

It burst inward with little resistance. A few feet away, Kris lay on the floor, hands tied behind her back, ankles bound. A man stood over her, face twisted in rage, a hammer raised over his head. Justice lunged, going airborne for several feet before sinking his teeth into the man's raised arm.

While others restrained the suspect and Jared called off his dog, Tony dropped to his knees in front of Kris, his heart twisting. Although she was still conscious, she looked as if she'd been through a boxing match. Her face was misshapen, and even in the poor lighting and shadows cast by those gathered, it was obvious the bruising was extensive. One eye was swollen completely shut, the other open only halfway. She released a moan and let that eye shut, too.

Tony looked back at the others. "She needs medical aid, pronto."

But Sanchez was already calling it in. Bella approached and sat in front of Kris, releasing a whimper.

She opened her eye again and tried to smile with swollen, blood-caked lips. Bella gingerly licked her cheek and whimpered again.

Kris shifted her gaze from her dog to Tony. "You came."

He swallowed around the sudden lump in his throat and took her hand in his. "You're safe now. I only wish we could have found you sooner."

He squeezed her hand, foregoing the hug he wanted to give her. Behind him, someone was reading the suspect his rights. Sanchez was still speaking with dispatch, and a conversation was going on between two of the SWAT guys.

But Tony's main focus was on Kris. She was alive, the only victim to survive abduction by this man. *Thank you, God.*

Her fingers tightened in his, ever so

slightly, and her eye drifted shut again. "How did you find me?"

"A former friend came forward, knew about this place from when they were teenagers."

But even Kenny's help wouldn't have been enough without Bella. Not finding either the pickup or the sedan, they'd finally stopped along 61 and headed into the woods. A short time later, Bella had picked up the scent, leading them in a slightly different direction.

"Without Bella, we would never have found you in time."

"Good girl." Her speech was slurred, her eyes still closed.

"Help is on the way." He squeezed her hand again.

She returned the gesture, or at least tried to. Her grip was so weak, it was hardly detectable. Her fingers gradually went limp.

Tony squeezed her hand. "Kris?"

No response.

He cupped her battered face. "Stay with me, Kris."

More of Sanchez's conversation drifted to him, words and phrases like "head injury" and "medevac."

"Hang in there, sweetheart."

God, please let her be okay. After saving her from a madman, they couldn't lose her to her injuries.

He'd cared for her since adolescence. Now he loved her.

Would he ever get the chance to tell her how he felt?

Should he?

Two hours later, Tony paced the surgical waiting room of Ascension Providence in Mobile. Kassie, Jared and his family waited with him. Robbie Sanchez had ridden from Pensacola with Jared and had agreed to take Kenny and both dogs back with him in Jared's cruiser.

Mobile had been hit as hard as Pensacola, but the lights were on here. Hospitals were always the first to get power restored.

After being carried through the woods on a stretcher, Kris had been airlifted to the hospital and rushed into surgery as soon as doctors had determined she had a skull fracture with bleeding on the brain.

He'd called his dad before leaving the cabin to ask for prayers. Instead, when he'd arrived, both of his parents, as well as Nick and Joanne, had been waiting for him.

Since then, he'd alternated between worrying and praying. He'd tried sitting a couple of times, but with all the pent-up anxiety, he hadn't been able to stay still. At this point, pacing suited him better.

The door to the waiting room swung open, and the surgeon stepped inside. Tony's heart seemed to lodge in his throat, and he suddenly couldn't breathe. It seemed like an eternity passed before the doctor spoke.

"She came through the surgery well and is resting comfortably. She'll be kept sedated for a few days, but we don't foresee there being any complications."

Tony's knees went weak, and he sank into a chair. *Thank you, God.*

The doctor continued. "She'll be in recovery for an hour or so, then moved into ICU. You can all go get some rest."

When they stepped into the hall, Nick fell in beside him.

"What are you going to do when she wakes up?"

"I'm hoping I'll be here."

"As a friend or something more?"

He slid his brother a sideways glance, one with a little bit of annoyance. They'd had this discussion several times already. Tonight, he was too exhausted to rehash it.

"You've fallen in love with her. I can see it every time you look at her."

"So now you've turned into a mind reader."

"I don't have to be a mind reader. It's all over your face."

Yeah, it probably was. It didn't matter. No matter how much he loved Kris, he couldn't bring himself to feel that he deserved fatherhood.

"Do you believe that God is in control?"

"Of course, I do."

"Do you think He'd somehow turned His back or gotten preoccupied, and Zoe died when He wasn't looking?"

"Of course not." He lowered his gaze to the floor. No, God hadn't turned His back, but Tony had.

Nick stopped walking to grab Tony's shoulders, then gave him a rough shake. "How long do you plan to keep punishing yourself for something that was completely out of your control?"

"I don't know."

Nick dropped his hands. "You need to let it go."

Let it go. Wasn't that what he had, in so many words, just told Kenny? It was easier said than done. Right now, he needed to be by himself and pray.

Nick moved ahead of him to catch up with Joanne, but Tony held back, hands curled into fists. Maybe his brother was right. Maybe he needed to take his own advice. Could he really let it go and leave the rest to God?

God, I need Your help. I can't do this on my own. Help me give this up to You.

A hint of something good stirred inside, a sort of release—a sense of freedom that was close enough to touch but too far away to grasp and claim. He'd held on to the guilt for fourteen long months, mentally beating himself up time and again.

He slowly uncurled his fingers, opening his hands. *God, take the pain, take the regret. Help me to release it all to You.*

An invisible weight seemed to lift from his shoulders, and he drew in a deep breath. Nick and Joanne didn't blame him. They hadn't right from the start. Nick had told him over and over to stop blaming himself.

He was finally ready to listen.

Determination surged through him. The next few days would seem like years, but as soon as Kris woke up, he'd tell her how he felt. Maybe she wouldn't be ready for anything more than friendship. Maybe she thought he'd make a lousy father and she'd be better off raising Gavin alone.

Whatever the outcome, he wouldn't leave her side until she knew exactly where he stood.

Kris drifted on a blanket of clouds.

She had no idea where she was but really didn't care. At least not enough to open her eyes. She was comfortable. And she was safe. For some reason, the latter seemed to really matter.

She drew in a deep breath and released it slowly. The clouds dispersed, and the surface behind her back firmed up. She wasn't floating. She was lying in bed, a pillow beneath her head.

When she opened her eyes, her surroundings were foreign. She wasn't in her bedroom. The ceiling was closer than her ten-foot ceilings at home, with fluorescent lights set in, currently off. A tall, narrow window that didn't appear capable of opening occupied part of the pale wall to her left. Where was she?

Memory rushed back to her and images flooded her mind—the rundown cabin, her captor standing over her, fists clenched, the hammer moving at lightning speed toward her head.

Her gasp sounded amplified in the silence of the room. A rustle nearby was the first sign that she wasn't alone. Her heart kicked into high gear, and her breathing turned to shallow pants.

When a familiar face moved into her circle of vision, the panic swirling through her subsided. Tony was there. But where was her son?

"Gavin?"

"He's fine. Kassie and Mildred are trading off taking care of him."

When she tried to smile at him, her cheeks seemed to resist the motion. Her lips did, too. It would take time for her face to return to normal.

"How long have I been asleep?"

He pulled out his phone and did some math in his head. "About eight hours... plus three days."

"Three days!" How was that possible?

"They had to do surgery and kept you

sedated afterward to give your brain a chance to recover."

"Have you been here the whole time?"

"Just about. I was off Sunday, and I'm using vacation time the rest of the week. That padded chair against the wall actually reclines and doesn't make too bad of a bed."

The thought of his remaining by her side almost continuously sent warmth flooding her chest. Granted, he was just a friend, but she couldn't ask for a better one.

"So, how bad do I look?"

"A lot of the swelling has gone down, but you're sporting some pretty interesting colors, from yellow to blue to purple to black."

"Can you find me a mirror? On second thought, I think I'll take your word for it." Maybe by the time she had to actually look at herself, a lot of the bruising would fade.

He eased down next to her and took her hand in his. "I should probably call for a nurse now that you're awake. I'm sure the doctor will want to check you out."

The reluctance in his tone told her he wanted to be alone with her now that she was conscious. She wasn't about to object.

"I don't think I'll die from neglect in the next few minutes."

"Good." He squeezed her hand. "Sometime when you're feeling up to it, I'll fill you in on the events leading up to your rescue. Lots of people were praying, and God answered. If not for a vacation ending just in the nick of time and a dog with a super sniffer, things would have turned out differently."

"I'd love to hear about it. I have to admit, I wasn't holding out much hope. When you burst through that cabin door, I thought I was seeing things."

"The more we learned, the more concerned we were. The killer had an older sister who abused him horribly when he was a young child."

"Lana."

He lifted his eyebrows and tilted his head.

"He kept calling me Lana. He was punishing me for everything she did to him."

He pressed his lips together. "In doing some checking, the authorities learned she disappeared from her home in Mississippi eight months ago. Her body was found a week later, her head smashed in with a hammer. Her murder is still unsolved. She was petite and dark-haired, just like all the women he abducted."

"He was arrested, right? He's locked up?"

"Yes. He'll pay for his crimes."

"Good." She would eventually be called on to testify. Having to relive the events of this past weekend wasn't something she relished. But Tony would be right next to her. She released a sigh. "I'm so glad it's over. For everyone."

She searched for the bed control and pushed the button to raise the back. A dull ache filled her skull, intensifying the more upright she became. She stopped at about thirty degrees. At least she wouldn't be trying to converse lying flat on her back.

"Have they identified the bones under the gazebo yet? That seems like forever ago."

"I just found out this morning." He hesitated, frowning. Sympathy filled his eyes, mixed with a lot of concern.

"It's okay. I'm pretty sure I already know where this is going."

He nodded. "The bones belonged to your mother."

Knowing what was coming didn't help. The news still ripped the foundation from under her. It was one more blow in a series of blows.

Their mother had loved them and hadn't left them by choice. But any sense of closure or other relief she may have felt was crushed by the knowledge that their father had killed her.

She turned her face toward the window and blinked back tears. Tony squeezed her hand.

"There was a suitcase buried with her."

She rolled her head back to the other side and looked at him sharply. "So she was planning to leave." It didn't take a genius to put the pieces together. She was packed and ready to run off with her boyfriend, her father discovered her plans, flew into a rage and killed her.

"She was going to leave, but she was planning to take you three girls with her."

"How do you know that?"

"She'd packed her journal. It was lying underneath her clothes, sealed up in a gallon Ziploc bag."

"You guys read it?" Her chest tightened with the sense that they'd violated her mother's privacy.

"Not me personally. I've been here with you. But, yes, the crime scene people looked at it. It's evidence."

"Will they give it back to us eventually?"

"I'm sure that won't be a problem when they're finished with the case."

She dipped her gaze to her lap. She'd been angry with her mother for so long, had even vowed that if she ever returned, she'd spit in her face. Now she wanted nothing more than to hold in her hands the book where her mother had poured out her heart.

"Your dad will likely be charged with murder."

"He'll never stand trial. They recently diagnosed him with stage-four liver cancer." It would be a sad end to a sad life. She paused. "What else was in the journal?"

"I just got a brief summary, but I know she wrote a lot about his drinking and jealousy and fits of rage, and that if he ever laid a hand on any of you three girls, she'd leave. Then she learned that he was engaged in some activities that could put you girls in danger. That was when she decided to take off with you."

He squeezed her hand again. "One thing was clear from everything she wrote. She loved you, all three of you. She wouldn't leave you by choice."

Kris remembered that day well, coming home from school to find her father in the kitchen, head in his hands, an open bottle

of whiskey in front of him. She'd instinc-
tively known something was wrong. Her
mother had never allowed him to drink
at home.

Kris had called out to him, and he'd
looked at her with puffy, bloodshot eyes.
A piece of paper had lain on the table in
front of him. She'd moved close enough
to read what was there—a note from her
mother.

She looked at Tony. "But she left a note.
I saw it. She explained that she couldn't
take it anymore, that she was going to
meet her boyfriend in the Bahamas and
run away with him. She said to tell us girls
that she was sorry."

"That totally disagrees with what she'd
written in her journal. Was the note hand-
written?"

"It was typed, but she signed it. I recognized her signature."

After reading the note, she'd run upstairs
to find Alyssa holed up in her room with
the door locked, refusing to let anyone in.
Kassie had arrived home a few minutes

later, shock dissolving to sobs when she'd gotten the news.

Tony frowned. "She might have left a note, but based on what she'd written in her journal, that wasn't it."

It was possible. Her father could have taken her signature from the note she wrote, typed his own and copied it with her signature at the bottom.

"Based on the journal entries, your mother was taking you three girls out of the home and leaving."

She drew her eyebrows together. "But she bought a plane ticket to the Bahamas. The information was on the credit card. Dad showed it to us. There was only one ticket purchased."

"Did anyone actually verify that she was on that flight?"

"Probably not. I mean, it wasn't treated like a homicide or even a kidnapping. Between the note, the proof of purchasing the plane ticket, her missing suitcase and clothes and Dad's claims that she'd been having an affair, it was pretty cut and dried. Not a stitch of any of our clothing was missing."

"She'd apparently gotten her own things packed but hadn't gotten to yours and your sisters' before your father caught her."

She drew in a sharp breath, a sudden hollowness in her stomach. "She *did* get our stuff packed, at least Kassie's. The next day, Kassie insisted someone had messed with her clothes. She said the stuff in her dresser drawers had been moved or gone through or something. Kassie was actually picky enough to have noticed something like that. But Alyssa and I thought she was nuts." She shook her head. "Mom didn't walk away from us *or* her faith."

Tony smiled. "She didn't."

"You said I was out for basically three and a half days. That would make today Wednesday, right?"

"Yeah."

"I don't suppose your church streams its midweek services."

"Nope, just Sunday mornings. Why?"

"I have a lot of catching up to do."

A smile spread across his face, even as his eyebrows rose in question.

"You may not have realized it, but you were getting through to me. I was softening. It was just a matter of time until I found my way back to the Lord. But last weekend's events sort of fast-tracked it. When I thought I was staring death in the face, I knew I wasn't ready to meet God. I've remedied that."

"That's awesome. I can't tell you how happy that makes me." He drew in a deep breath. "Recently, I've had some realizations of my own. Ever since the day we got paired up searching for Julia Morris, I've been fighting feelings for you, trying hard to not let what there was between us move beyond friendship."

She could relate. She'd been fighting the same war and had thrown up the white flag of surrender the day he and his family had helped her secure her house. Maybe she was finally ready to admit it.

Her lighthearted tone hid the turmoil inside her. "How has that worked for you?"

"Not too well. It's pretty much been a losing battle." He once again grew serious. "When I discovered you'd been taken, and then hour after hour passed with no leads, I was so afraid I had lost you, and I kept thinking about how I'd never told you how I feel."

He reached across her lap to take her other hand and squeezed them both. "I'm not asking for anything. No decisions. No commitments. And maybe my timing on all this stinks. I mean, a few days after you've had brain surgery probably isn't the best time for me to unload a bunch of heavy stuff, but I just want to let you know that I love you, and not just in a simple friendship way."

As she looked at the affection shining from Tony's eyes, her heart responded. Everything she'd tried to hold back rushed forward, bursting through the floodgates.

And it was okay. Her feelings for Tony no longer felt like they were dishonoring Mark. He'd want her to find love again. She was young and had her whole life ahead of her. He'd also want a good man to be there for their son, to step into the role of father.

And there was the problem. Tony would never be that man, not because he couldn't, but because he wouldn't.

"What about Gavin?"

"I love him, too."

That wasn't what she meant, but his answer was still sweet. "We're a package deal, you know."

"That's a pretty awesome package, I'd say."

Did he really mean it? Loving her little boy and taking responsibility for him were two different things. If he wasn't going to be in it for the long haul, they needed to step right back over the friendship line and forget this conversation ever happened.

"We've discussed your feelings about kids before. What changed?" Or had anything changed?

"My brother gave me a stern talking to at the hospital. It wasn't his first. Like a lot of big brothers, he has a tendency to stick his nose in where it doesn't belong. But this time, I listened. The thing that happened with my niece, he said I need to let it go. Since I'd given someone else the same advice a few hours earlier, I thought it would be best if I listened."

"Funny how that works. So you're not afraid anymore that he's going to snap in two or self-destruct?"

"I'm trusting God to keep him in one piece."

"So am I." And it felt good. She'd been doing life on her own for far too long.

He squeezed her hands. "I would love to kiss you right now, but with what you've been through in the past few days, it probably wouldn't be a pleasant experience."

He was right. It hurt to even try to smile. But how many times as a teenager had she dreamed of a kiss from him? She wasn't about to pass up the opportunity now.

"Stop making excuses and kiss me."

A grin spread across his face, and he leaned toward her. When he was close enough for her to smell his aftershave and feel his breath against her mouth, he hesitated, giving her that three-second pause to change her mind. Then he closed that final distance between them.

His lips met hers, his touch featherlight, and warmth exploded inside of her. He'd been wrong about it not being a pleasant experience. He released her hands to softly cup her face. Even with all the care he was taking, those teenage fantasies hadn't done the real experience justice. Not by a long shot.

All too soon, he pulled away. "I love you, Kris, and I promise there will be more of those to come."

"I love you, too. And I'm going to hold you to it."

"I hope you do."

He released her one hand and leaned back in the chair. "By the way, Kassie's planning a graveside service for next week. She's already contacted Alyssa and says she wants both of your input."

"That sounds good." Her mother was finally getting the burial she deserved, recognition for a life well lived but tragically cut short.

The day would be bittersweet—the public acknowledgment of her love for them, a long overdue goodbye. And Tony would be right by her side.

But she had one more thing to do before paying her final respects to her mother. She had to confront her father.

She'd been hurt and angry before, the hatred for her mother something she'd thought she would carry till her dying day.

She wished she could say that anger was gone. It wasn't. It had only been redirected. Now her father was bearing the full brunt of it.

Killing their mother was unthinkable.

Letting them believe she'd abandoned them was cruel.

Perpetuating that lie for the past ten years, knowing what it was doing to each one of his daughters, was unforgivable.

TWELVE

A steel gray sky hung heavy over the small group of mourners gathered in St. Michael's Cemetery. Concrete monuments topped with crosses rose high above the typical grave markers, and family mausoleums stood stately among graves dating back to the 1700s.

Small cement borders segregated some sections. Others were walled off by fences of wrought iron. In one of those walled-off sections, a funeral tent stood in front of a gold-colored casket, a spray of lilies, carnations and Monte Cassino asters on top.

Kris sat in the front row of cloth-covered chairs, Kassie on one side of her, Tony on the other, his fingers intertwined with hers. Gavin sat in his lap. A monument in the center proclaimed that this section belonged to the Singleton family. Her mother's parents, grandparents and great-grandparents were buried here, as were several aunts, uncles and cousins two and three times removed.

Kassie's pastor stood next to the casket, an open Bible in his hand. Actually, he was Kris's pastor, too, now that she'd returned to her roots. He'd just finished reading Psalm 23 and was currently offering words of comfort to the family and friends.

Jared sat on the other side of Kassie, and Tony's parents were in the row behind them. Nick and Joanne, too. A couple dozen people from their church stood outside the canopy, people who had known and loved their mother.

Alyssa was conspicuously absent. Kris wasn't surprised. Disappointed, yes, but not surprised.

According to Kassie, their younger sister hadn't wanted to be involved in the planning and had told Kassie that she'd be fine with whatever she and Kris did. But they'd both expected her to at least show up.

Kris drew her attention back to the pastor, who looked up from his Bible. "Wherefore comfort one another with these words."

Tony squeezed her hand, offering silent comfort. Someone started singing the first verse of "Amazing Grace," and others joined in. Kris sang along in an undertone, leaving the musical people like Kassie to carry the tune.

A few days ago, she'd gone to visit her father. She'd learned her mother's death was an accident. Her father had come back to the house to get something shortly after leaving for the charter office and walked into their bedroom to find her filled suitcase on the bed. She'd been in the bathroom gathering up her toiletries.

He'd known then that she was leaving and had slapped her hard across the cheek, knocking her to the floor. She'd cracked her head on the edge of the bathtub and lost consciousness immediately. Within minutes, she'd begun to convulse and died. He hadn't meant to kill her.

At least, that was what he'd claimed. She was inclined to believe him. Maybe that was because, although he'd been verbally abusive, he'd never seriously threatened any of them. Or maybe it was because believing her death was an accident was easier than accepting the alternative.

The volume of the voices rose coming into the last verse, and the atmosphere became almost celebratory. *When we've been there ten thousand years...*

Her mother was gone, but Kris had no doubt where she was. She hadn't walked away. Her faith had been as genuine the day she died as it had been throughout their childhood.

She couldn't say where her father's heart was. He'd seemed truly sorry for everything, had even asked for her forgiveness. She hadn't been able to give it. Not yet. Eventually, she'd have to. God would require no less.

The verse ended, and the pastor offered

a closing prayer. After lying in a crude grave at the water's edge for ten years, her mother's body would soon be lowered into its final resting place.

She'd asked her father about that, too, how he'd managed to bury her without any of them knowing. He'd said that he'd hid her body in the detached garage until late that night. Then he'd dug the shallow grave, carried her out and covered her up, well before the first hint of daylight.

At the pastor's amen, Tony released Kris's hand to rise and position Gavin on one hip.

Kris stood, too, and held out her hands. "I can carry him."

"I don't mind."

Gavin didn't seem to mind, either. He'd wrapped both arms around Tony's neck.

"Besides, you're in heels."

She was. She was also wearing a dress. It was a rare occasion when she put on either. She'd even applied makeup, equally rare. It had completely hidden the last remnants of bruising. When he'd arrived to pick her up and she'd met him at her front door, his eyes had lit with appreciation. Maybe she should dress up more often.

After the friends attending had offered their condolences, Tony took her hand with his free one and walked her toward the gate where they'd entered the cemetery. Nick and Joanne walked ahead of them, Kassie and Jared beside them. Tony's parents trailed behind.

Kassie released a sigh. "I feel like I can finally shut the door on our troubled past and start fresh."

Kris nodded. "Me, too. It's like a new beginning."

For the first time in months, the future looked bright. She'd been given the opportunity to say goodbye to her mother and remember her with fondness and love. She still had work to do in reconciling with her father, but going to see him was the first step in that process. It wouldn't be her last visit.

Mark was gone, and after a year and

a half of almost inconsolable grief, she'd finally begun to heal. It was all because God had put Tony in her life. She couldn't say for sure where things would end up, but she was happy with where they were headed.

Joanne turned around to smile at them. "We're looking forward to a new beginning of our own."

Tony's steps faltered. "Are you saying what I think you are?"

Joanne's smile widened. "We didn't want to say anything until I had passed my first trimester. But everything looks good, and about the middle of next February, we think we'll be welcoming a little boy into our family."

Tony released Kris's hand to wrap Joanne in a one-armed hug. "Congratulations, sis. That's awesome news."

Tony moved to the side to congratulate his brother, and Kris hugged Joanne. "I'm so happy for you. You guys deserve this." She released her and stepped back. "Gavin will have a little playmate." Gentle and sweet, he'd be good with a tiny one.

After all the congratulations had been given, Tony put his arm around her, and they moved toward the arched entry. He squeezed her against his side. "I'm ready for my own new beginning. Today is the first day of the rest of my life, and I want to spend every day of it with you and this sweet little boy of yours."

She craned her neck to look up at him. Her heart began to race. Did he mean… what else could he mean with a statement like that?

"Are you asking me to marry you?"

"I guess I am."

"Then I guess my answer is yes, although I can't believe you actually proposed in a cemetery."

"We're not in the cemetery anymore."

"Okay, we're two feet outside the gate."

He winced. "Really romantic, huh? I guess I didn't plan that very well."

"It's okay. I'll give you a do-over. And you'd better make it good. Candlelight dinner, getting down on one knee, the ring—the whole shebang."

"It's a deal. I'll even get Jared's and Nick's input so I don't blow it." He turned her to face him. "I'll do it right later, but I think even this sorry proposal needs to be sealed with a kiss."

She grinned. "I couldn't agree more."

He leaned toward her, Gavin still propped on one hip, and slid his free hand behind her neck.

When his lips met hers, the warmth that flowed through her had nothing to do with the balmy August afternoon. She wrapped her arms around him, Gavin in the circle. They were a family, permanent and complete.

A horn blew, and they broke the kiss to watch a pickup truck holding a couple of high schoolers drive slowly past, the passenger leaning out the window whooping and hollering.

Tony let out his own whoop. "We just got engaged!"

The truck kept going, and their families

moved closer until all nine of them were pressed into a big group hug.

Kris smiled. "If Mom could look down from heaven and see us right now, she'd be happy."

Tony returned her smile. "You think she'd approve?"

"Without a doubt."

As she stood in the small press of bodies, her heart soared. She'd wondered what it would be like to be a part of a family like Tony's.

Now she knew.

She wasn't just part of a family *like* Tony's. She was part of Tony's family, and it was awesome.

She looked over at Kassie and smiled.

Even her own family was turning out to be pretty good.

* * * * *

If you enjoyed
Sniffing Out Justice,
Be sure to check out
Kassie and Jared's story,
Searching For Evidence,
the first book in the
Canine Defense series
by Carol J. Post!

Available now from
Love Inspired Suspense.
Discover more at LoveInspired.com

Dear Reader,

I hope you've enjoyed Kris and Tony's story. This is the second book in the Canine Defense series set in Pensacola, Florida.

We got to know Kris as a grieving widow in the first book in the series, and it was fun reconnecting her with her high school crush. Tony and Kris both had a lot of trauma to work through before they could reach their happily-ever-after. Kris didn't believe she would ever love another man the way she had loved her husband, and the death of Tony's niece while in his care convinced him he would never be a worthy father. But if we just let Him, God has a way of mending broken hearts and creating beauty from ashes.

Be on the lookout for the next and final book in the series, where Alyssa reunites with her first love.

May God richly bless you in all you do.

Love in Christ,
Carol J. Post